Adios Muchacho

Adios Muchacho

Burn in Hell

Joe Race

Order this book online at www.trafford.com
or email orders@trafford.com

Most Trafford titles are also available at major online book retailers.

Author photo by Juanita Mendoza

Printed in the United States of America.

ISBN: 978-1-4269-5692-8 (sc)
ISBN: 978-1-4269-5693-5 (e)

Library of Congress Control Number: 2011902024

Trafford rev. 02/04/2011

 www.trafford.com

North America & International
toll-free: 1 888 232 4444 (USA & Canada)
phone: 250 383 6864 ◆ fax: 812 355 4082

Other Books by Author

Movin' On
Ramblin' On
Continuin' On
Hawaiian Paniolo
Moon Over Manila
Floater on the Reef
Sitting on a Goldmine
Christmas in the Tropics
Korean Shadow (Children)
Adios Muchacho – Burn in Hell
Shrimp: The Way You Like It (Cookbook)
Stories from Wild Bill's Bar & Grill – (Anthology)

Dedication

"As always to Miss Salve' of Laguna…ang aking kaibigan, asawa, kasama, at minamahal…"

"Ever-cheerful, ever-helpful, ever-knowledgeable, ever-editing – if the words pass muster, I get an **OK**, and if not, the very long explanation is **NOT YET...**"

Acknowledgments

Salamat po, kalangen, and *muchas gracias* to that usual band of merry outlaws, "the ones that rode hard, worked long and never slacked off" that kept me going with their ideas and editing: "Cowboy" Jeff Williams, Urbano Duenas, Walt Goodridge, Billy Oregon, Donna Liwag, Bud White, Ronnie Mandell, "Yuma" Danny Hocking, "Argonaut" Johnny Bowe, Russ Mason, and of course, all my wonderful family members.

While writing this story, I enjoyed the Great State of Arizona for all its exquisite beauty, history, and wilderness, and of course, the fine citizens with a very unique blend of Hispanic and Anglo cultures.

I appreciate the support and encouragement from my island friends, and especially enjoy the 'walk-about' time on the beach. An hour on the Lau-Lau Beach with the old-timers under a swaying palm tree will break a "writer's block" every time.

And a major *mahalo* to my devoted dealers – the purveyors of hearty French roast dark coffee – Gresil and Sylvia. Bless you my children!

And very importantly, thanks to my loyal readers – your monetary considerations keep me supplied with rice, papaya, barbequed chicken, fresh veggies, and Tinian hot sauce.

Contents

Adios Muchacho – Burn In Hell

Uno

Luke Quinn woke slowly to the melodies of the larks, wrens and chickadees punctuated by the occasional squawking of a restive blue jay. He looked upwards into the pine trees and saw a family of squirrels bounding back and forth on the branches. Sunlight filtered through the lower aspen leaves which were already turning golden with the beginning of autumn. A cricket was chirping in the soapweed. He had ridden long and hard the day before, and he felt like he needed another few hours of rest.

Listening to the soft rhythm of the nearby stream as it rolled over small rocks, he pulled a blanket up over his head to make-believe it was still night. But his horse Charger and his dog Perro were not going along with the program. They were used to getting up at daybreak, being watered and having their morning fodder, and on the trail by seven o'clock. His horse kicked up dust and small rocks back and forth and Perro made little whiny noises, and he knew they were watching every movement of his blankets. He could feel their eyes burning into his back. They made so much racket that Luke finally gave up and crawled out of his blankets. He moved the hobbled Charger to the stream where the noisy animal slurped up the water and munched on the stream grasses. He gave Perro the left-over beef and stew from the night before.

He built a fire to make his Arbuckle coffee. He was hidden back in the evergreen forest and was using dry wood, and wasn't concerned about the light-grey smoke from the fire attracting the attention of marauding outlaws or renegade Indians. Besides he had Perro with him, fully able to pick up every sound and smell in the forest. He broke out several hardtack biscuits and a few strips of beef jerky for his breakfast. He washed it down with coal black coffee just the way he liked it.

Luke was a tall and lean man. He was pushing the half-century mark but still had all his hair, mostly graying, and a big bushy mustache. His body could read like a history book of his past escapades – stabbed and scarred several times, and a gunshot wound to his right leg and one through his chest muscles that missed his heart by fractions of an inch. He had recently retired as the first of the US Deputy Marshals out of the Denver District and wasn't particularly looking forward to being a rancher; but he had promised his father he would take a look at the family ranch.

Within an hour, Charger was saddled, the fire doused, and they were on their way to somewhere on the outskirts of Tucson where Luke had inherited a hundred square mile of ranch property from his father after his unexpected death. Supposedly the ranch was hidden away in the foothills and the lawyer letters told him that "you can't get there from where you are in Colorado." There were no railroads or stage coaches that crossed the ranch property. The lawyer suggested that he come to Tucson and hire a guide to take him to the boundaries of the open range and the ranch house, and maybe take along a wagon-load of supplies.

The lawyer also said most of the cattle on the ranch had either strayed off or were rustled by one of the many marauding gangs in the area. Occasionally the local Indians would separate out a few for feeding the tribe. Overall, there were apparently hundreds missing. He added that oftentimes, the cattle were driven off across the border into Mexico. Apparently his father had become incapacitated, and had only kept a few old and loyal hands on the payroll, several of them living in line shacks miles away from the main ranch house. Branding and castrating of the cattle hadn't occurred for several years, and it was nearly impossible to identify and separate a wild animal from one belonging to the ranch. The local sheriff hadn't done much to stop the rustling. The area was so vast and he only had five deputies.

It was also reported that his father, Jesse Quinn, had married a Mexican woman, and that she still lived on the ranch. The lawyer had told Luke that the woman wasn't making claims on the property – she just wanted to return to Mexico City after he showed up to take over. She had promised Jesse to make sure the ranch got turned over to Luke.

Dos

As Luke worked his way through the thick brush leading to the valley, he heard what sounded like gunshots, maybe several dozens from various caliber firearms. He was usually the first into battle, and it was no different now that he was a retired law enforcement officer. It was just part of his personality and his training to meet problems, even gunfights, head on.

He rode Charger along the top of a ridge leading to the gunshots. Charger was sure-footed and Luke didn't worry about the rocks and gravel that his hoofs were kicking up. He felt his horse become totally energized, prancing and snorting, and he saw that Perro was excited running alongside the horse. The hair on his back was standing straight up. He had been taught to stay behind Luke, unless he received the command to directly move ahead. The horse and rider, and Perro moved as one unit. Luke heard more shots and yelping Indians.

Luke peered over to the next valley, and saw that two men in Mexican white peasant garb were holding off six Indians on horseback. He saw that the Indians, appearing to be Apaches, were circling the two men who had taken cover behind two massive boulders, but they were becoming increasingly vulnerable as two of the Indians jumped off their horses and were making an assault on foot behind several clumps of saguaros. One Indian, apparently already dead, was lying prone in front of the men, his rifle several yards in front of him.

Luke removed his rifle from his scabbard and took definite aim at the first of the Indians sneaking up on foot behind the men. His shot hit the mark and the Indian fell forward. He knew that his shot would encourage return fire, so he pulled his horse behind several juniper bushes and moved on foot about thirty feet at an angle which would give him an excellent shot at the other Indian on foot.

Perro was on full alert and ready to move but Luke ordered him to stay. Neither the Mexicans nor the Indians would take kindly to a charging ferocious dog and Perro was likely to be shot by both sides.

After the Indians had vamoosed, Luke approached the two Mexicans carefully from behind large boulders that had rolled off the mountain, not wanting to be shot because they were jittery and far into the survival mode. He yelled out from his cover that he was he was a friend.

The older Mexican yelled back, "Come out from behind the rock and keep your hands in plain view." His English was spoken clearly, close to the perfect King's English.

Luke raised his hands and broke cover, holding his Winchester rifle high in his right hand. He said, "I'm a retired Federal Deputy US Marshall. I'm your amigo. I have my bonafides in my jacket pocket."

"Come forward slowly."

"I'm putting the rifle down and reaching inside my jacket."

Still at gunpoint, Luke took out his bonafides and walked slowly towards the Mexican. "The identification will tell you who I am. Can you read English okay?"

The Mexican took the identification and perused it quickly. He asserted, "Of course, I can speak English. I went to school in England for three years."

"Sorry, I didn't mean to insult you. I just thought you were crossing into the US to look for a better life."

The Mexican paused and said, "We'll talk about all that later. Right now, I have to take care of my nephew. He's been shot twice but it appears that the damn holes are only flesh wounds."

Luke whistled up his horse, and took a shirt out of the saddle bags. He tore it into strips, and placed a pressure bandage on the wounds, and wound them tight with the remnants of the shirt. He said, "The bleeding has stopped. He'll be okay but it's a long way to Tucson for him to ride a horse. I see the Indians took your mounts."

"Yeah, they did. Too bad - they were strong Spanish horses. But we still have all our personal gear and saddles." He took out a tequila bottle from his bedroll, and gave the youngster a shot for the pain and splashed a few dollops on the wounds. He added, "Gracias for helping, amigo. I saw a stage coach going north yesterday. If we're lucky, we might be seeing the coach on the return trip. Let's go over and walk along the stagecoach route in the direction of Tucson. Can you stay with us until the coach returns? Never know about the Indians coming back."

As they walked, Gregorio explained that they had come to Arizona to find a certain ranch where his mother had worked for many years as a housekeeper and wife for an old man. In the last letter, the mother had said that she was temporarily retiring on the ranch and her husband had built her a cozy cabin to last out her days if she decided to stay.

The Mexican said, "My name is Gregorio Isaacs, and the boy is Frederico Isaacs, my nephew. He goes by the name of Freddy. We got to Tucson a few days ago and asked for directions and somehow, we ended up here, too far north. We planned on going back south in the morning but then the Apaches hit us. We heard from the townspeople that they jumped the San Carlos Reservation along the Gila River."

"That's an unusual name for a Mexican. What part of Mexico are you from?"

"Everybody always asks. My father was a Jewish merchant from Austria. He sold anything and everything. He met my mother while he was doing his selling rounds in Mexico City. They fell in love, got married, and I was the result, the oldest child. They also had a girl several years younger, my sister, who is Freddy's mother. She fell in love with an American sailor, got married, became pregnant, and he left on the next ship out of the harbor. We never heard of him again. Two years later, she fell victim to cholera. Freddy kept the Isaacs name, and he moved in with us. He's been like a son to me."

Luke asked, "Where's your father now? Is he back in Austria?"

"No, he died. I had a wonderful childhood, and often sailed back and forth to Europe. Father placed me for about three years in an English boarding school, where I learned to speak English properly. On one return trip to Europe about ten years ago, his merchant ship *Carmen de Acapulco* sailed directly into the whirling jaws of a Caribbean hurricane, and that was the end of the ship and my father."

"Did he leave a nice inheritance for your mother to survive?"

My mother Carmen tried her best to sort out my father's business ventures. He had left no written instructions and his partners were all uncooperative and greedy, and mainly based in Austria. So... we were left penniless. My father wouldn't have wanted it that way but the partners had many advantages over her. She wasn't able to read the many contracts and dealings, mostly written in Austrian. They even secretly raided the accounts that my father had in Mexico, and everything else was hidden away in Europe.

"During these tough emotional times of a year that dragged on seemingly like forever, my mother met an older American rancher who needed a housekeeper and cook. The rancher had dropped off a herd of cattle in Mexico and was taking a much needed vacation in Acapulco. I met the man and liked him. My mother did also, and within four months they were lovers. Mother agreed to accompany him to Arizona, but only if I could go along, along with Freddy."

"And did you go?"

"Freddy wanted to go. But I only had one year left at university for my dentistry degree so I declined saying that I would catch up later. My mother kept trying to persuade me to go, and when I decided not to go, Freddy chose to stay in Mexico also. He had learned English and was already working part-time for several companies as a translator."

"Wow, that put your mother in a bind. Losing her husband, and then one year later, her two closest relatives decided to stay in Mexico, and she is off to an unknown ranch in Arizona."

Gregorio answered "Yeah, it was a tough decision, but the rancher convinced her to go and we had a great, celebratory wedding. He promised that she could visit Mexico City every couple of years to see her family and friends. He was good to his word, and she visited four times with the rancher along on the first two visits. On her third visit, she said the old rancher was too sick to travel, and on her last visit, she declared that he had died. She said that she would stay on until the rancher's son showed up to take over the ranch. Her husband had built her a cozy little cabin on the side of beautiful creek shaded by huge cottonwood trees."

Luke said, "This is sounding like too much of a coincidence. What was the rancher's name?"

"I always want to say Quinines, like in Spanish; but it might have been simply Quinn."

"First name Jesse? Like Jesse Quinn?"

Gregorio smiled and said,"Yeah, that's it, Jesse Quinn."

"Jesse Quinn was my father. Looks like we're both heading for the same ranch."

"Looks like you just saved your stepbrothers. Now, all we have to do is find that stagecoach."

"Yep, and find your mother and the elusive ranch."

Tres

Their talk was interrupted by a cloud of dust coming down the trail. Both men tensed, and Freddy said, "Give me a gun. Looks like the bastards are coming back." His speech was slurred – the tequila was having its pain-easing effect. He wouldn't be able to hit the side of the largest barn in the county.

Luke smiled. He was happy to see that the lad was always ready to stand his ground.

As the dust got closer, they recognized the outline of a pack of mules and a stage coach. The coach stopped about a hundred yards away. The steel-tired wheels of the Concord created a thick screen of dust and small rocks which slowly settled to earth. It apparently hadn't rained in many months.

Luke said, "Likely the driver is trying to figure us out. Just raise up your arms so he can see that we aren't carry firearms…like we're not threatening." Luke put down his rifle against a rock.

After they raised their empty hands, the stagecoach slowly drew closer. Luke could see that man riding shotgun was old and grizzled, but very determined at protecting the driver and coach as he pointed the eight-gauge scattergun straight on at the trio. There was a male passenger sticking a snub-nose revolver out on the right side window from the interior of the coach. He looked like some kind of traveling salesman, even wearing a bow tie in the wretched desert heat. The coach had the name *Hawkins Stage Lines* stenciled along the side.

The coach moved closer.

Luke's attention was immediately drawn to the ash blonde driving the coach. From afar, the driver wasn't immediately identifiable for her gender. As the coach drew nearer, he could see that the driver had her hair pulled up inside a tobacco-brown Stetson. The flat-crowned hat had a band made from rattler skin. Up close was another matter. Even though covered with trail dust, her skin was soft and feminine, and her eyes matched the blue of her denim shirt. She wore tight-fitting jeans and wore a gunbelt carrying a .45 caliber pistol with plenty of ammo.

Luke opened his wallet and showed her his identification and badge as a retired deputy marshal. He held the bonafides high. Luke introduced Gregorio and Freddy and said that they needed to get the young man to a doctor as he had been wounded by the renegade Apaches.

The driver introduced Gus, her shotgunner and the salesman inside as Rafael Goodman. She said, "I am Abby Hawkins, the owner of the stage line." She hopped down from the stage. When she shook hands, Luke noticed she wasn't wearing a wedding ring. She said that she had to stretch her legs, and make a quick stop behind a thick bush. As she walked away, Luke noticed that she had an hour-glass figure with a very shapely bottom.

Gregorio was also watching Abby walk into the bushes. He said, "Yes, she is a pretty one, but much too young for you."

"And for you. This is a crazy situation. She's only about thirty, young for us but too old for Freddy."

Gregorio chuckled, "Or maybe she in love with the old shotgunner."

"Or maybe the sleazy salesman. He told me that he sells ladies' expensive "unmentionables.""

"No male competition here, but possibly she has a lonesome cowboy at either end of the line."

Luke replied, "No competition, eh? Getting white on top but still plenty of heat in the old boiler."

"Yeah, you're right. Improbable but not impossible." He stroked his mustache and silently mouthed, "Oh, la-la. Here she comes."

When she joined them, Abby talked about the pesky Indians, and amateur outlaws who had had been trying to hold them up on almost every run. She hadn't yet lost a mining payroll or any of the US mail. The whole situation would have been hilarious and amateurish except the attacks had become tragic when one of her shotgun guards had been sniped off and on another run, a driver had been shot. Consequently she was having a tough time rounding up people to help – most had been scared off or gone to work for other lines. She had to start making the run herself because the employees had decided her route was too dangerous. She said the old guard aboard was on his last run. He attributed the resignation to rheumatism but she knew he wanted to live out his last days in the shade of a big cottonwood tree. Several of her best mules had either died or been stolen from the corrals. She was close to bankruptcy.

Abby agreed to transport the stranded trio into Tucson. They loaded Freddy into the coach and laid him across one of the benches set up for three passengers. They heard him sigh and he was soon off to slumberland. Gregorio sat next to the salesman, opposite of the wounded victim. Luke chose to ride on top with the luggage and strongbox. Abby said that it would be a good idea to stay alert and be ready for anything. The last robbery attempt had been only five miles from town.

Luke and Gus checked their weapons and had extra ammo ready. They worked out a plan that he would shoot to the right and Gus' side was to the left. This allowed them each a definite angle of fire and also kept them from shooting each other, or Abby, as the coach bounced along and the gunfights might become mobile, moving from side to side.

Perro ran along side the coach for several miles, and then Gregorio reached down and pulled him inside. The ride to town was uneventful except for the occasional loud cries from Freddy whenever they bumped a large rock or hit a deep hole. The coach stopped at Doc Haggerty's clinic, and luck was running Freddy's way. The doc was in his office and cold sober. He took a quick look at the lad's wounds and made what sounded like a good "hmmm."

Once on the operating table, Doc observed that both bullets had gone right through the victim and the direct application of tequila on the wounds seemed to have stopped any signs of infection.

Doc said, "I'm going to keep the boy here for several days just to watch for infection and make sure the healing is happening on schedule."

Gregorio replied, "Gracias, Doc. Much appreciated." He then asked, "You know a good hotel that would be willing to take in two old cowboys?"

"Just try the Widow Carson's boarding house down the way about three blocks. She's got nice clean rooms and serves up delicious meals. I often eat there myself."

Luke queried, "How about a stable for my horse? And do you suppose the widow will take kindly to me bringing my dog to the house?"

"Stable is on the way. I think the widow will take in your canine. She's got several dogs herself for protection. She'll take the dog if he's willing to be friends with her mutts."

"No problem there, Doc. Perro just gets a little anxious if I'm threatened. He's not too territorial – generally willing to compromise."

Doc said, "Well, have a good visit. Widow Carson is a wonderful woman. Be nice to her."

As they strolled to the stable to board Charger, Gregorio said, "I think I heard a little love interest from the doctor about the widow."

"I think you're right. Maybe he eats his breakfast with the widow-woman."

Cuatro

The widow, Joanna Carson, was more than happy to rent two rooms to Luke and Gregorio, and after a few sniffs and snarls, Perro was also welcomed into the household.

Joanna was a joyful soul and a large woman. Her ample figure rippled with every movement. She wore her hair in a large bun, and she was constantly sweeping her gray hair from her face and pushing the hairs back into place. Luke noticed a loaded shotgun near the back door.

The boarding house had plush burgundy drapes, white lace curtains, and thick, green potted plants in almost every room. The wallpaper was a design that you might see back East in a mansion along the Hudson River and there was even a pair of crystal chandeliers in the main dining room. The table was made from rosewood, and the chairs from sturdy spruce. For evening meals, the widow put out embroidered napkins and placed silver utensils and bone china at each setting.

Gregorio and Luke were shown their clean and spartan rooms. Joanna explained the meal times and arrangements, and said that the evening meal would be ready in about an hour. She told them that her Indian housekeeper was preparing baths in two different rooms. She said to leave the soiled clothing out for the housekeeper and that the clothes would be freshly washed.

After Joanna had left, Luke couldn't help himself, and said, "That's one big woman, maybe Scandinavian. Best not cross her 'cause she can beat your ass."

Gregorio answered, "I do believe you are right. Maybe that's why the doc drinks. He must be stressed out knowing that he has to send Joanna to paradise every night. That would be a major workout."

"And she is a widow. Maybe the husband's heart just gave out."

"Thank goodness, she's a happy person and likes to help."

The Indian housekeeper, Alyce, appeared and told the men that their baths were ready. Luke's bath was only a few steps from his room. After Alyce got Gregorio settled in for his bath, she returned to Luke and told him to strip down and leave the dirty clothes at the door. She looked him directly into his eyes. Her huge doe-eyed expression didn't change. She was beautiful, young, with a moon-shaped face, and could still be considered a virginal Indian maiden.

Luke asked, "Are you going to leave?"

"No, unless you want me to? I will help you bathe."

"Okay with me. Is this part of the room service?"

"No, it is my idea. When I saw you, I knew you were a nice person. You were polite and respectful of Mrs. Carson and to your friend."

As Luke began to take off his clothes, his male member decided to do its dance. He hadn't been with a woman for several months. She noticed and said, "Not to worry. I'm a married woman and know what to do. We can settle him down."

Luke eased into the water. It was the perfect temperature, and Alyce began to wash him with lavender soap. She started with his hair and worked her way across his back and chest. The water splashed several times, so she stood up and stripped down to only her pantaloons. Her breasts were bare and symmetrical, and standing proud. He saw hints of stretch marks on her abdomen, and asked, "You're a mother?"

"Yes, a baby girl. Her name is Margarita and she lives with my mother on the Navajo Reservation. My husband ran away about a year ago and may be dead in battles with the Long Knives or other Indian tribes. He is a Navajo and there have been many fights with the Apache."

"How did you get here?"

"I went to the reservation school and learned to speak English. One of my former teachers heard about my problem; she told Mrs. Carson and I got this job. I've been doing it for over a year. She's a very nice woman."

Luke smiled and asked, "And do you treat all the guests with this friendly service?"

"Oh, no. I am a church girl but have become very lonely. So I have decided not to stay pure for my husband – he may never come back, and my urges are getting stronger every day. I had a dream last week that I mated with a Caucasian man. I have a strong itch."

"And I showed up. Very convenient for you and for me."

She asserted, "Now stand up so I can wash your other parts." She washed his feet and legs, and then washed his buttocks. She was not a shy girl and washed every corner and hole of his backside.

She said, "Now, turn around so I can wash your little soldier." When he did, his erection almost slapped her in the face. But she took command, washed it thoroughly and slid it into her mouth, while still washing his testes. He erupted almost immediately.

In a very matter-of-fact way, she rewashed him, patted him on the butt, and said, "It's almost dinner time. Mrs. Carson has put robes out for you and Gregorio. She told me that it's okay for you men to wear robes this evening for dinner, but from now on, she expects you to be fully-dressed in clean clothes and on time. Dinner is served promptly at six o'clock."

As she was dressing, Luke asked, "Will I see you later?"

"Yes, after ten o'clock. I have to do all the clean-up and complete some preparation for breakfast. I will come to your room." She gave him the slightest smile.

The boarders came down for dinner at the proper time. Gregorio had poked into his saddle bag and changed from his white peasant clothes to a combination of tight black jeans, a light blue shirt and high stovepipe riding boots. He looked every part the successful, prosperous Spanish cowboy *vaquero*. Joanna and Alyce were impressed with his appearance. Even Rafael threw out a compliment when he said, "Now, that's what a cowboy should look like."

Dinner was an epicurean delight, especially for being out in the middle of the Arizona desert. Doc showed up right on time. The underwear peddler, Rafael, had also booked into the boarding house and as a salesman, had the gift of gab and told stories of questionable veracity. Mrs. Carson and Alyce served up a large salad, followed by beefsteak *au jous* and trout served in dill sauce. The guests were treated to a carbohydrate choice of potatoes, rice and fresh bread and tortillas. Dessert was fresh-baked cherry or apple pie.

After dinner, the men retired to the large living room. Alyce brought out a decanter of brandy and glasses, and offered one to each of the men. Luke broke out his supply of dark Madura cigars that he had shipped in from Cuba. The men lit up and the conservation was lively. Doc assured Luke and Gregorio that Freddy was doing fine and not to worry. The nearby café was taking care of his meals.

Doc and Rafael strolled out to the veranda with Mrs. Carson. Luke took the opportunity to ask Gregorio if his bath was memorable, that is, did anything special happen? Gregorio looked puzzled. He replied that the water was pleasurable and warm, and that he finally felt clean after five days on the trail.

Luke asked, "Nothing else?"

"No, nothing else. The bath was wonderful. Alyce said she would wash my clothes. She also volunteered to wash Freddy's also. Geez, what are you talking about?"

"Nothing at all." Luke was secretly happy that Alyce had not spread her charms around indiscriminately. He was looking forward to his evening soiree –he snagged an extra decanter of red mountain wine.

Doc and Gregorio strolled over to his clinic and found that Freddy was sitting up eating his meal from the café. A young woman was in attendance, probably all of fifteen years old. He told Gregorio in *Espanol* that he shouldn't worry, that he wouldn't do anything stupid with the young lady and get them chased out of town.

Rafael went to bed early. On returning from the clinic, Doc sat and slowly read the newspaper. Luke and Gregorio borrowed a few books from the bookshelves and retired to their rooms. Within twenty minutes, Luke heard Rafael and Gregorio vigorously snoring from their rooms, like two freight trains building up speed to clear the mountain. It had been a long day.

Then, he heard what sounded like Doc creeping up the creaking stairway and heading towards Mrs. Carson's large bedroom. Just before ten o'clock, he heard Joanna coming up the stairs and heading for her room. Luke chuckled to himself. He thought to himself that the couple was adult and experienced, yet they were still concerned about appearances, that somehow the self-righteous element in society would condemn their love affair.

He heard his doorknob turn and a promise of heaven floated into his room. She was wearing a white night robe but underneath, hardly anything at all. She had bought a transparent pink nightgown from Rafael. The gown blended beautifully against her mahogany skin. She stood in front of him, and he gently massaged every angle and corner of her magnificent body. She had trimmed her pubes. As she sat next to Luke, the noise from the main bedroom indicated that Doc and Joanna were giving the springs on their bed a serious workout.

Alyce laughed and said, "They do this every night. I don't know how Joanna can stay so fat. They're always humping like bunny rabbits. I have to change the sheets every day."

"No wonder you get so horny, hearing that every night!"

"You're so right, my cowboy. Now Marshal, come arrest your Indian gal. I have been very, very bad."

"Duty calls."

Cinco

Next morning at breakfast, Luke and Gregorio learned that the Quinn Ranch, better known as the *Triple Q* (3Q brand), was a huge spread of land, but the eastern section contained the ranch house, which was only thirty miles away. Luke explained to everyone at the table that his father Jesse had included three generations of Quinn in his brand (his father James, him and Luke). He had written a dozen letters to Luke inviting him to come down from marshaling in Denver and take over the ranch. Luke had written back and said that he still had so much to do in catching the bad guys. There never seemed to be an end to the outlaws. The prisons were full and the gallows busy.

But Luke knew now that he had waited too long, that his father had died. But he was now anxious to see the land, and meet his stepmother, Gregorio's mother Carmen. He still wasn't sure that he wanted to be a rancher but he was willing to take a look.

Through Joanna, Luke and Gregorio found a reliable guide and managed to find a horse to rent for Gregorio. Perro, sensing the excitement, was waiting at the front gate of the boarding house. Charger was raring to go. The stableman had fed him well, and brushed him until his coat was black and shiny. They stopped off to see Freddy at the clinic, and he was ready to go on the ride but Doc nixed the idea, saying he needed another couple of days before he could get on a horse. He sat on the front porch of the clinic and watched the three riders and horses disappear over the horizon.

They came to a fork in the road, and right away, Gregorio knew that he had previously taken the wrong road to the right. The guide Carlos pointed to the left. Gregorio said to Luke, "What the hell, if it had gone well, I might never have met you. I could have packed up my mother, and we would be on the way to Mexico by now."

"And we wouldn't have met Abby."

"Oh yes, sweet Abby. If we get back in time, I might have to pay her a visit."

"What are you going to do, Mr. Dentist, check her teeth?"

Gregorio smiled and replied, "In a fashion, I would think. She probably needs a checkup and a thorough cleaning."

"I'm thinking she might need a good security agent, or some one to keep her company on the long rides back up to Phoenix. My English W. W. Greener eight-gauge is all loaded and ready for service."

"Mi amigo, I know what kind of service you have in mind."

"That's true. It would be just a part of the overall service, no extra charge."

The taciturn guide finally talked when he said, "We are almost there. Just a mile or so past the little ridge in front of us. The ranch house sits in quiet valley with year-round water from mountain springs and run-off."

Gregorio whispered to Luke, "See, I told you he could talk."

The trio crossed the ridge and dropped down into the wide green valley. The hills were covered with a dozen varieties of cactus such as cholla, ocotillo, Spanish bayonet, and yucca. Sage, purple lupine, ragweed, goldenrod and dozens of other plants dotted the landscape. It was an enviable location for anyone to live and prosper. A few cattle were spotted grazing at the grass along a gentle creek that flowed down the center.

Luke approached the ranch house with some trepidation. Even though they yelled ahead, no one came outside to greet them. The house looked dilapidated, and parts of the barn were falling in. There were no chickens or ducks in the yard, and no dogs or other animals moving about. It was eerie and lonely but Luke remembered that his father had told him that he built a cabin for Carmen. He figured there would be a cabin close by. There were no directions or notes at the unlocked house.

Luke proposed that they spread out in three directions, and if any one of them found anything, they could fire three shots in quick succession. Gregorio agreed to the plan. He now looked concerned about his mother, wondering where she could be, and if she was still alive. He had experienced first hand the violence from the Indians, and had heard tales about marauders from Mexico and Texas. In the best scenario, he figured she might have gotten impatient and headed home to Mexico on her own. He also knew the inner strengths of his mother, and was hoping that she hadn't tried to stop a passel of rustlers on her own. He knew she often had a shotgun with her and a tiny .32 caliber revolver.

Luke gently touched blunt spurs to Charger's flanks, and said, "C'mon, boy. Let's go find my daddy's wife." Perro trotted along at the big black's heels, yipping his determined bark.

After about an hour, three shots were fired from Gregorio's direction. He had built a smoky brush fire so that the other two men could easily find his location.

When Carlos and Luke reached Gregorio they found him resting on the porch of a well-cared cabin made of natural logs. He was sitting on a bench next to an older Mexican woman.

As they approached, he waved them over and jubilantly declared, "This is my mother Carmen. She is alive and well." He paused and added, "And as beautiful as ever. She is doing okay but is ready to return to her hometown in Mexico."

Gregorio made the formal introductions. Carlos excused himself and said that he would see to the horses. Carmen explained that Luke's father had battled a deteriorating heart ailment which eventually turned to pneumonia. Doc had been out to the ranch house several times but Jesse didn't improve. Jesse put his remaining ranch hands to work building the cabin which Carmen could maintain until Luke showed up to take over. Carmen said that it had always been Jesse's desire that Luke give up law enforcement and become a rancher.

She continued, "Luke, your father worried about you all the time fighting the outlaws. He always dreaded that the sheriff might ride out with a sad message from Denver."

"Yeah, I know. He told me many times in his letters, but ranching never appealed to me, even as a young man trying to figure out what to do after college." He paused and asked, "How's the ranch doing anyway. It looks deserted. We heard most of the cattle have been run off or stolen by Indians, Mexicans or marauders."

"I'm afraid that's true. I haven't been tending to the ranch, and I haven't seen our line hands in several months. They usually stay out in one of three line shacks. A general delivery man brings out my supplies and food every two weeks, and he hasn't seen or heard of the three drovers either. Their names are Bob in the west shack, Monte in the north, and Gabe down south. I don't know if they're alive or dead, or maybe run off with the outlaws. I never liked Bob – he always seemed like he could go bad if the price was right."

Luke asked, "How do we find the shacks?"

She answered, "Not easy. Each one is about a day's ride. You can circle them all in about two days. I know an Indian boy that helps me out. He's been to all the shacks. He'll be here tomorrow - he checks in every Monday."

Luke said, "Well Gregorio, looks like we'll be out for a few days from town. The girls will just have to wait."

Carmen interjected, "Tell me about these girls. Do you guys both have girl friends?"

"Gregorio is just dreaming. He's got his eye on the beautiful woman that runs the stagecoach line."

"I heard about her. Really gorgeous and very strong and independent. From what I hear, any man would have a tough time getting her under control."

"Just an easy challenge for Gregorio. He fancies himself quite the Latin lover."

"I suppose it runs in the family. That's what your father said about me."

Just then they heard a rifle shot. All three of them scrambled for their weapons. They noticed that Carlos was gone, but not for long.

He came walking up the front pasture with a young buck slung over his shoulders.

Luke laughed and said to Gregorio, "I believe I know what we're having for dinner. Get out your skinning knife. I'll start a barbeque fire."

Carlos spoke again, for the second time on the trip. "I couldn't resist. We were hungry and there he was, sent by the Great Spirit."

Seis

Carmen fixed breakfast next morning, complete with fresh eggs from her chickens, and sausage from the townsman who had arrived with her weekly supplies. Hussong, the Indian boy, also showed up. He said that he knew where the shacks were and could take time to show Luke and Gregorio where they were. Carlos decided to stay on. On his return to Tucson, the townsman agreed to deliver messages back to Mrs. Carson's boarding house, and to Freddy at Doc's clinic.

Carmen packed up enough supplies for two days for the men. Gregorio double-checked her guns to make sure they were in working order and that she had plenty of ammo.

The men reached the first shack at day's end. They hadn't seen one cow the entire day or crossed any human trails. The weather-beaten wooden shack was empty. The line-rider Monte was missing. There was no note and all the food and utensils were gone. There were moccasin footprints, and hoof prints from unshod horses around the shack. Luke asked Hussong, the Hopi, "Indians were here?"

Hussong replied, "Looks like it...maybe four ponies. The prints are fresh, since the last rain, and the shack has been empty a long time. The riders were probably just curious."

Luke decided it would be good place to bunk down. Hussong said that if they got an early start the next morning, they could see the other two shacks while circling back to the main ranch house. The men ate a cold dinner but Gregorio managed to get a fire going and made a passable pot of coffee. The tequila bottle was passed around afterwards, and Hussong took a slug on the first round, but avoided any more. His head was already clouded from the strong cactus juice.

The men sat around the fire outside the shack, sang and hummed a few old cowboy ditties. A hungry owl hooted from the dark depths of a tall bristle-cone pine. His continuing hooting elicited a frightened scurry of kangaroo rats, lizards and other natural prey of the swivel-headed predator high in the trees above. A coyote howled in the distance. The moon had set a few short minutes before, and the stars and planets began a swirling display of Mother Nature.

Perro lay down near the outer reaches of the shack. He was quiet, and so were the horses. If a mountain lion or a two-legged critter had gotten close, the animals would have let the men know, so the travelers slept soundly.

At daybreak, the men had their breakfast, saddled up and were off at a fast clip for the second shack. The shack's rock foundation came into view by noon. This was Bob's line shack, and he, too, was gone. The shack had been burnt to the ground. Neither of the shacks had any evidence of recently dug graves, and if the bodies had been left in the open, the animals would have left some evidence of their feeding spree, like old, broken bones and chewed-up clothing.

Luke said, "This is definitely becoming a mystery. What the hell has been happening?"

Gregorio responded, "One thing for sure, this ranch is too big to keep track of the cattle or even the drovers." He paused and added,

"There are two cattle hides over in the shade drying out. They're branded 3Q."

Hussong said, "There's no sign of any ponies since the last rain."

Luke asserted, "Let's get going to the last cabin. Maybe Gabe is still there and has some ideas what is happening."

Within two hours, they were in sight of the third shack. They heard several shots fired, and when they looked over the knoll, three concealed cowboys were blasting away at the cabin from barricades of old logs and boulders. There was an occasional shot from the shack.

Hussong said, "Gabe is not one of the three men firing from outside. He must still be inside."

Luke replied, "That makes it easy to choose sides. Let's just meander down on foot and have a serious talk with the shooters." They hadn't been spotted yet. Believing they could be seen by Gabe from the angle of vision, Hussong stood up in full view and waved a large handkerchief. Hussong was known by Gabe, and soon he stopped firing.

One of the yahoos yelled, "Hey, he stopped firing. Maybe we got the old bastard."

The three shooters relaxed, looking at the cabin and one of the yahoos carelessly exposed himself. There was another rifle shot from inside the shack, and the shooter slumped to the ground.

Another of the shooters shouted, "Shit, he got Leroy dead center. He's not moving."

The other shooter started to move and said, "I'm going around the back. I'll start a fire and smoke him out. If you get a shot, kill the bastard. He's going to die for shooting Leroy."

As the shooter made his way to the back of the shack, Luke suddenly emerged from the bushes and stood in his way. While he had been walking through the woods gathering brush for the fire, the shooter had placed his revolver back in its holder. His arms were full of wood. Luke held his Bisley Colt .45 revolver at belt level and told the shooter to put his hands over his head.

Luke noticed the man's eyes twitching and his arms shaking. He was deciding what to do. Luke cocked his revolver and said, "You don't have to die. Drop the wood and surrender." Luke knew from experience to be ready, and his instincts were right again. To be an outlaw, you didn't have to pass an intelligence test or need basic common sense.

The foolish shooter threw his armload of wood at Luke and went for his gun. Luke slightly raised his revolver for a heart shot, and eased back the hammer. As often like before, everything seemed to happen in slow motion. Before the shooter could center his handgun on his target or touch the trigger, Luke tightened his finger on the trigger and the hammer fell. Because of experience and training, the surging adrenaline didn't hamper the process. Smoke and flame gushed from the muzzle of his .45 and the sound of the discharge slapped back at him. The shooter grunted but continued to raise his weapon.

Luke knew he had to finish him off. With a coolness that belied the rapid pounding of his heart, Luke fired again. He saw the shooter's head snap back slightly and a smoking spray of blood and brains erupted out the back of the shooter's head. He was dead before his body hit the ground. Luke had killed before but the emotional trauma always stayed with him for a few days.

Gregorio yelled over, "Are you okay?"

"Yeah, I'm fine but had to kill the stupid SOB. I wanted to talk with him about what the hell was going on with the ranch."

"You can break cover. We've got the other jasper tied up. We'll yak with him. Gabe is coming out of the shack. He knows about you over there, so he won't shoot. We'll send Hussong and Carlos over to help with the body. Thank goodness we had Hussong with us – no friendly fire killing anyone. He's broken bread with Gabe many times."

When Luke joined Gregorio, he saw that the remaining shooter was just a youngster named Billy Jones. The kid was tall, skinny, and rat-eyed, with yellow, decaying teeth. He fit the image of a slinky, lying scoundrel that large cities seem to birth from poverty and broken families.

Gregorio piled all the yahoos' shooting irons and ammunition on a blanket under a tree. He commented, "These guys were really well-armed with quality weapons. Most cowboys can't afford guns like these. Someone is financing them for sure."

Luke asked, "Now Billy, why don't you tell us what's going on, or we'll just hang you from the massive oak tree?"

He answered, "I don't know nothing. I just rode with these guys to help with the cooking and chores."

Gabe said, "Screw him. He was shooting at me right along with the other two. I've got a rope inside the shack. We can string him up or save him for the sheriff, and let the sheriff hang him. Whatever you decide, I'm open. He's only about 150 pounds, and the rope and branches won't break."

Luke replied, "Makes sense to me. Carlos, go get his horse. Gabe, you can get the rope."

"Shit, you guys are serious. You're really going to hang me. I didn't kill anybody."

"How about the other drovers at the line shacks, like Bob and Monte?"

Billy sniveled, "I had nothing to do with those guys. Bob joined up with us, and he went with us to get Monte. I was only doing chores. Bob called Monte out of the shack, and the other guys shot him dead.

Then one of the outlaws shot Bob in the back. He said, 'You can't trust traitors.' We put both bodies in the shack, and lit it on fire."

Luke then asked, "Who's the big boss? Who's behind this whole mess?"

"I don't know. I'm serious. I don't know! I just went to work for these guys 'cause I needed a job. It's everything about cattle and shipping them to Texas. They mentioned that some business mogul wanted control of the Q3 Ranch because it was so big and had plenty of good graze and steady water."

Billy saw Gabe throwing a rope over the branch of a sentinel oak, and forming a hangman's noose. Billy's eyes grew wider and he made a high, whimpering sound. It was a pitiful, wailful noise. Salty sweat ran from his forehead into his eyes and he blinked dozens of time. To his dismay he couldn't get them to stop watering. Tears coursed down his cheek and he tried to stifle a moan of despair at seeing Carlos arrive with a horse. Hussong tied his arms behind his back.

Billy knew they would set him on the horse and after applying the noose, slap the horse on its flanks; and he would be left dangling and dying. He couldn't believe his life would end so soon. He screamed, "You can't do this. I want to live."

Luke calmly said, "You should have thought about that before you joined this killing pack of mongrels."

Gregorio stepped over and said, "Let me talk to this pissy little jasper. Maybe I can get him to spill the beans, to talk the truth."

Gregorio eased him away from the group, and sat him on a large fallen log. He asked, "Let's get to the right information. If you come clean, we'll save you for the sheriff and the courts. There, you might have a chance."

"Yes, yes, I'll tell you everything. Those guys want to hang me right now!"

He slapped the young outlaw in the face several times. The miscreant started crying in earnest and was close to hysteria. "So…you little puke. Tell me the truth."

"Okay, don't hit me again. I've been riding with these yahoos for about two months. We stole just about every cow we could find on this ranch and shipped them to Texas. The cattle broker and rancher is Timothy Leighton from Phoenix. He's what you call a cattle baron and already owns lots of New Mexico and big parts of Arizona. He wants it all. He's got other groups of yahoos working other areas, trying to scare away the owners. Some of the gunsels are from Texas and show no mercy."

"And what else?"

"They knew that the old lady in the main ranch house had a relative coming back to take over the ranch. The word was all over the territory. The plan was to take care of the line shacks, and then burn down the main ranch house. If she refused to move from her cabin, they would do what was necessary."

"And what was necessary? What do you mean?"

"They would pull her out of the cabin and if she refused, just burn that place down."

"Even is she was there inside?"

"The guy that Gabe shot was the ringleader. He said he wouldn't show the old lady any mercy. He said he would kill her and leave her for the buzzards."

"You were planning to go along with this?"

"No damn way. I stopped for water one day at the cabin, and she fixed me a big lunch. I was planning on leaving in a few days. I have enough money saved to get me to California. You can check my saddlebag."

Gregorio asked Hussong to check the saddlebag. There was $227 inside.

Gregorio tied Billy to a tree, and he and Luke took a walk to decide what to do.

"Look, I think the little jerk might head for California and that would the end of him in Arizona He's not real bright – he's a follower, and maybe next time he'll end up on the right side of the law. The question is should we take a chance on this fool? I told him that he if he came back to Tucson, there would a *Wanted: Dead or Alive* flyer on each store front and post office in the territory."

Luke stated, "Look, it's against my better judgment. He's either righteously scared or a damn good actor. Because he's young and mentally dull, maybe we can take a chance. Give him the cheapest revolver with five rounds, and the slowest damn mule, and have Carlos start him in the direction of California.

Billy cringed and backed against the tree. Gregorio pulled out his Bowie knife and cut the rope holding him to the tree. Luke grabbed him by the scruff of the collar.

"Aiyee, are you guys going to cut me?"

Luke said, moving his face within six inches of Billy, "Not right now, but if you ever come back to Arizona, we're going to cut you, shoot you, and then hang you from a rafter for the vultures. You understand?"

"Yes, thank you, Sir. Can I keep my money?" He then said, "You've let me live so I feel obligated to tell you - there's four or five more of Leighton's bunch out here in the hills."

"We'll watch for the nimrods. You'll get all your money, an old swayback mule and a cheap little .32 caliber revolver. That's for protection. Carlos and Hussong will accompany you out west for about five miles, give you the gun and money, and you best keep moving."

Gregorio added, "And if you rejoin the crooks and come back our way, I will personally gut you from your neck down to your balls! Understand?"

Billy shuddered. "I understand. But that little gun isn't much protection against the Apaches."

Luke interjected, "Quit whining. Get out of here before I change my mind. You best take a chance on the trail before we string you up right now."

"I'm leaving now. You won't ever see me again!"

As they left, Luke said to Carlos and Hussong, "If the little puke gives you any trouble on the trail, blast him and leave his carcass for the coyotes."

That elicited another conversation with Carlos, which was "humph," which Luke assumed was, "Okay, I understand."

Luke, Gregorio and Gabe went about the grisly business of burying the two outlaws. Gabe recovered a new shirt and a wide-brimmed hat from the bodies. He said he liked the coordinated colors.

Carlos and Hussong re-appeared as the burial detail was finishing up. They each took a back-up handgun from the outlaw's arsenal. The leftover rifles and shotguns were smashed and destroyed over the nearby boulders. The extra horses were turned loose, and the saddles and tack placed in the line shack.

Luke told Gabe to ride with them. There was no sense in manning a line shack when there weren't any cattle to watch.

Hussong said, "We can still get back to the ranch house by twilight."

Gregorio smiled and said, "I hope Mama Carmen has a huge meal for us."

Siete

They reached the ridge overlooking the ranch house just as the sun was setting. The men smelled smoke and when they crested the ridge, they could see that the main ranch house was totally engulfed by flames. Three riders carrying torches were going up the trail to the cabin.

Carlos yelled, "Don't worry. If we stay on top of the ridge we should get to the cabin before they do. Ride hard, amigos."

Luke agreed and said, "There's enough light that we can still move fast. Hussong and Carlos, I want you cowboys to go up the trail after the riders, and when we surprise them on top, we'll chase them right down to your little trap."

The moon ducked behind some clouds, and the last several miles were rough going through the brush and thick forest. It was uncanny how the horses wove their ways through the forest, surefooted and able to see in what was almost total darkness.

As they neared the cabin, they observed that it was dark and black. Carmen had apparently doused all the lights. The outlaws started blasting at the doors and windows, and one of the gunsels tried to approach the cabin with a torch in hand. He was highly visible from the flames, probably thinking it was safe to quickly advance, and believing there was only an old woman inside.

Several gunshots from different calibers stopped the outlaw in his tracks. He fell on his torch and was soon afire. Luke asked, "Wonder who's in there with your mother? There are at least two shooters, maybe three."

When the other outlaws heard his screaming, they broke cover. One of them yelled, "It's only an old woman. Let's kill her and burn the cabin to the ground." They opened up with rifles, shotguns and their revolvers. Luke, Gregorio and Gabe hit them hard and fast from the right flank. One of the men went down quickly, while the other managed to get to the porch, only to find Carmen greeting him with double blasts from her Parker ten-gauge shotgun. His facial expression was one of total surprise being shot by a female senior citizen but died before he could utter a word.

Gregorio yelled, "It's us, Mama. We're coming in."

"Good, *mi hijo*. You better get in here fast. Freddy's been hit."

Luke looked at Gregorio, and said, "Did she say Freddy?"

Gregorio ran to the porch. Freddy was lying near the front door and had been hit by one of the outlaw's shotgun blasts. He seemed only to have several pellets in his left side, maybe from a .00 buck shotgun load. He was going to make it…again!

Gregorio asked what he was doing there. He said that he had left town after sneaking away from Doc and arranged to be escorted out by Carlos' younger brother, Tomas Rivera. He said that Tomas had been shot just as the two opposite parties converged on the ranch house. He said that the outlaws just started firing at them. There was no palaver. They had no idea what the deal was. Tomas hid in some bushes and told Freddy to continue up the trail and at the top he would find the cabin and Carmen.

Gabe said that he would head down the trail and find Carlos and Hussong. The moon had re-appeared from behind the clouds and the going was much easier. He announced himself to the two men, and they soon answered. The search then began for Tomas. They heard some soft moaning and found him hiding in small cave. He was in bad shape. He had lost a lot of blood, and he was hot and sweaty from the beginning of a fever. Being young and strong was in his favor.

Gabe volunteered to ride to town and find Doc. Carlos and Hussong fashioned a rustic travois and pulled Tomas up to the cabin. The men laid him in bed, and Carmen carefully washed his wound. About half of his left shoulder had been traumatized but no vital organs had been damaged. His heart and lungs appeared intact. He was in severe pain. From experience, Freddy knew the dynamics and value of the pain medication called tequila. Carmen had a large bottle in the pantry, and it worked, and Tomas soon fell asleep, as did Freddy, who somehow managed to take a second dose.

Gabe found Doc right where he expected he would be; just about ready to give the widow's bed another major work-out. He told Doc that they had to travel fast, that there were two shot cowboys at the 3Q. As Gabe saddled up the doctor's horse, he could hear Doc making his goodbyes, and explaining that he would be back in eight to ten hours. He grabbed his doctor's bag and scooted out the door.

The Indian housekeeper, Alyce, whispered from the shadows, "How's Luke? Is he okay?"

"Yeah, he's fine. Go back to sleep. We'll try and get back by noon tomorrow."

Once on the trail, Doc said, "Gabe, it'll be a long night, but it's mighty peaceful under the stars, and away from that wild woman."

"Doc, you need to go through your doctor's bag and slip something in her tea at night. As we get older, we need our rest."

"Yep, you're right. Being ravaged every night knocks the hell out of a man's libido. Laudanum might do the trick."

Ocho

At daybreak, the men dragged the three dead outlaws 100 yards into the forest. Hussong asked, "Should we bury these bad white men?"

Luke answered, "You know, I'm tired of burying these evil bastards. We'll he heading for Tucson in a few hours. Salvage their guns and bullets. We'll let nature's forest creatures take good care of the carrion. Let the shit be recycled."

Hussong inquired, "Do you want their personal belongings, like identification for their families, and two of them had money and pocket watches?"

"Finders-keepers. It's all yours. They're probably all runaways and the families are likely relieved that they're gone from home."

"We'll keep the horses and use them for pack animals to get Carmen and her favorable belongings to town."

Gabe and Doc arrived just as the two gunshot patients were waking up. Freddy was wobbly but managed to find his balance on his first two steps. He said, "It might not be the wounds. I maybe drank too much tequila –my head is bursting."

Tomas just laid back and smiled as Doc cleaned his wounds. Doc asked, "How are you feeling?"

"Fine, Doc. A lot of pain but glad to be alive. I never figured out who those outlaws were. I raised my arm in greeting and they just started shooting at us."

"I've giving you some pain-killer medicine. It will take effect in about fifteen minutes. Regarding the gunslicks, we think they might be rustlers working for a man named Leighton in Phoenix. He favors himself some kind of land baron."

Tomas drifted away without another word. He was still grinning, probably hallucinating or thinking about how glad he was to be alive.

Carmen went all out for a scrumptious breakfast. She figured that they would be leaving for Tucson so why not clean out the pantry. She laid out rashers of bacon, with scrambled eggs and flapjacks, fresh milk from the family cow, and a bottomless pot of strong, aromatic coffee from Mexico. Freddy was doing okay – after three helpings, it was apparent that his appetite had definitely started anew.

After a morning cigar, the men sat around the large living room of the cabin, and decided their next move. Luke said, "We need to start for town and get our wounded lads into a safe environment."

Gregorio laughed and said, "I know what safe, warm environment that you have in mind. Doc told us that your little Indian maiden was asking about you."

"You've got that right. In between gun battles, I've been thinking about her firm young body, and her long black hair. I dreamed about her last night for the second time." He then asked, "And did Abby send you a message, that maybe she wants to see you soon?"

Gregorio playfully punched Luke on the shoulder, and said, "I know she desires me. I just have to get to town and make her realize how much she wants me."

Luke said, "Carlos and Hussong have already agreed to make a stronger, padded travois for Tomas. It will be rough going for the lad but Doc can fill him up with laudanum. We can't leave anyone here in cased another bunch of the hired killers show up."

Gregorio asked, "What about the cabin? Any number of renegades could show up and torch it? You could use it if you decide to rebuild the ranch."

"It'll possibly burn but right now we've got to get the lads into town for finishing up their medical treatment and get Carmen to a safe haven."

"Bet you don't put Mama up at the widow's boarding house. That could create some questions from Mama."

"Thank goodness, Doc has a neighbor lady that will take Mama in for a spell."

Luke laughed and said, "You best be careful with gossip. The old ladies will be talking about you courting Miss Abby."

"Jehoshaphat! I've got to be careful."

"What is that word, some kind of Austrian exclamation?"

"Nope, just an expression I've learned from the American west."

The men agreed to pack up and leave right after lunch. The noon meal, a gourmet's delight, was spectacular: beef broth, venison tongue, wood-duck, and potatoes and wild rice. Dessert was a tart of fresh cherries, followed by brandy and more black coffee. Luke felt his waistline expanding and knew now what his friends with a wife or steady girlfriend, called "the married look" (contented but going to fat). He decided he would skip dinner.

Afterwards, the group walked up about two hundred yards to the grave on the mountaintop and solemnly said goodbye to Jesse Quinn, Luke's father. Carmen took down the small cross, and the men covered the grave with rocks and pine needles. They wanted the grave site to blend in with the environment and didn't want any passersby digging away out of curiosity or greed.

At the cabin, Carmen loaded up two horses until they almost dropped at the knees. She placed the cross on top of the stronger animal. There were many memories and treasures to take away. Tears were in her eyes as she thought back about all the good times before Jesse got sick and they weren't hassled by rustlers and renegade Apaches. Gregorio patted his mom on the back and gave her a big hug.

He said, "We're off on another adventure. That's what my father would say, and I know Jesse would also. You're a fine woman and the road may well take you back to your old home in Mexico."

The travel to Tucson was slow but steady. On one of the inclines, the travois turned over and dumped Tomas out on the trail covered with decomposing, slippery granite. He howled in pain, and called Brother Carlos a series of expletives, mostly in Spanish. Doc reached in his magic bag, and said, "Time for another pain-killer." Within minutes, Tomas was back again enjoying his ride to town.

The men noticed Indians several times silhouetted against the sky on the mountain ridges. Hussong said, "Apaches."

The Indians didn't advance or threaten, but Luke and Gregorio pretty much figured that the cabin was a goner. The Indians knew the old lady lived at the cabin alone and she was in the group going to town. It was good time to return a white man's home to the soil.

Nueve

Scuttlebutt circulated through town that Luke and Gregorio would be coming in from the ranch about sunset. Abby prepared one of her Concord coaches to meet the men and bring the wounded back to Doc's clinic. She took the dirt road as far as it would go in the direction of the ranch and waited for the travelers. It was a colorful evening, could even be considered romantic, as she intermittently thought of Luke and Gregorio. She knew that she liked them both, in many ways.

About an hour before sunset, the string of horses and riders headed her way. She tightened the reins on the mules and turned her coach so that it would be heading towards town.

As Luke joined Gregorio at the head of the travelers, he said, "Do you see who I see? Do you suppose she rode out here to see me or her fantasizing Latin lover?"

"No doubt Abby wants to see me."

"Or maybe she's a good Samaritan and wants to help Doc and the wounded."

Gregorio smiled and said, "Whatever the case, I like a woman that likes to help others. She might need a sweet massage today with special Eucalyptus oil. I have some in my bedroll that I use for sore muscles."

It was a greeting of celebration. Hugs and introductions went all around. Freddy managed to get in the coach on his own. Abby said, "If you keep riding like this, I'm going to have start charging you for the rides. You're just using a few bullet holes as an excuse.

"Abby, it's a deal. As soon as I'm better, maybe I can work for you, be a hostler and take care of the animals."

"Sound good to me. Looks like Tomas is in pain."

Freddy laughed, "No problem. Here comes Doc with some more laudanum. Tomas will probably be giggling in a few minutes."

The men loaded up Carmen's valuables on top of the coach. She rode inside the coach with the wounded lads. Doc told Abby where to drop Carmen at his friend's house on the way to the clinic, and then leave the wounded lads at his office. At the last minute, Abby nodded at Gregorio and gestured for him to ride up on the driver's box. He tied his horse on the back of the coach, and like a little school boy gleefully in love, jumped up on the coach alongside Abby. He mouthed to Luke, "Don't wait up for me, my brother. I may be late."

She saw him making the facial expressions, and added, "You never know about us cowgirls."

Luke waved and in a cloud of dust, said, "Good luck, you two. Have a great evening. See you at breakfast. We gotta make some plans in dealing with Leighton."

Luke went back to the boarding house and let Mrs. Carson know he was alive and would be showing up for dinner. Even though he said he would skip dinner for the bulging waistline, he justified a good healthy meal based on his busy day. She asked about Doc and wanted to know if he would be back for dinner. Trying to cover for his exhausted friend, Luke said that he had two wounded young men and that he might have to stay at the clinic.

She said, "I'd better get down there with some food for the three men."

"No, that's okay. Doc arranged for some food from the café."

"I might just go down there after dinner to make sure everyone is comfortable. By the way, Alyce is drawing your bath. She saw you coming down the lane."

In a conspiratorial manner, she whispered to Luke, "The lingerie salesman is still here. He's selling a lot of bloomers and nighties to the town's married ladies and also some to the whores at the 'Painted Palace.' He went down there last night with his case of dainties and hasn't been back since."

"Maybe he made a friend or two."

Joanna gave her heartiest, lustful laugh and declared, "Maybe he took it out in trade. I just hope Doc comes back tonight –I miss him awful." She then winked, "And Alyce bought another nightie – the new one is lavender. Wonder who it could be for, eh?"

"See you at dinner." He gave her a big hug and headed up the stairs to his room.

Alyce was waiting for him. His bath was ready and so was she. After quick dip to wash off the trail dust and grime, Alyce asserted, "Mrs. Carson said I could help you with your bath for about forty minutes before we start dinner. We've already wasted five minutes. Let's go – I have a new nightie."

"No time for that. I've been thinking about you for three days."

Sitting on his bed, he watched her disrobe. She sat next to him, and they kissed deeply and with a boiling fervor. Luke probed with his tongue, and she responded, setting up a lingual duel, parry and thrust, engage and disengage, lunge and ripost. He was soon in her with his lance and they began to surge and grind, giving and taking in equal portions, like experienced lovers. They knew they were on a time limit, and they moved faster and faster, and as the ultimate joy arose, they slowed down to savor the exquisite sensations of a mutual release.

At the last incredible moment of friction, they tore their lips apart and their eyes locked. Alyce was the first to speak, "Oh my gawd. Waiting for you to come back sure built up my desire."

"Me, too. You have touched my soul. I saw stars."

"I saw stars too. Not really, I saw way more. I saw the big constellations of the universe. Part of me is still out there!"

"I'm happy that you're happy. I think we need some sustenance for later tonight."

"You're right. I have to get to work. Tonight we're having meatloaf from a recipe that Mrs. Carson inherited from her grandmother. It is beyond delicious."

"Gracias for the bath and the welcome-home party. I'm going to take a little nap while you're slaving away in the kitchen."

"You better rest up. I'll be visiting after ten o'clock, that is if you want me."

"You better come back. After all that riding, my butt needs a massage."

The meatloaf was served with baked potatoes and carrots, water cress salad, and fresh-baked apple pie with cheddar cheese on top. At the last minute, Gregorio and Abby showed up and asked if they could join the group for dinner. Abby said that she couldn't dream of eating at a restaurant when Joanne's meatloaf was on the menu. Doc and the lingerie salesman were among the missing.

Abby sat next to Luke and listened to his every word and laughed at his jokes. Gregorio and Alyce were noticing their attention to one another, and were mostly left out of the conversation. Being an Indian, Alyce remained quiet and passive but several times her big shiny eyes flashed a little anger. Gregorio kept trying to get Abby to leave but she said she wanted to hear more about the ranch. Joanna served a large bottle of homemade dandelion wine in an ice bucket as a cordial, and filled a dainty tulip-shaped glass for every one. Alyce left to make some herbal tea. Abby left for the toilet.

Gregorio said, "What the hell are you doing? Are you trying to court Abby?"

"No interest at all. I have my sweet little maiden."

Joanna added, "It doesn't look that way. You've spent the whole evening yakking back and forth with Abby." She looked at Gorgorio,"Maybe she's just trying to make you jealous. I've never figured out how people's minds or emotions work."

Gregorio answered, looking at Luke, "We're going to drink our wine and then move on. I don't expect that you'll be asking her to stay longer."

"Got it amigo. I wanna move upstairs anyway, and good luck with your woman."

Alyce returned with the tea. Everyone declined except for Abby. She took a full cup and also a glass of wine. She continued to talk on everything from the stagecoach business to the ranch. Alyce left to clear the table and do the dishes. She was mumbling blurred words to herself, and as Luke watched her go, she shrugged her shoulders.

Luke yawned several times, and said he was tired. Abby kept talking until finally Gregorio said, "We should let these people get some sleep, and don't you have an early stagecoach run tomorrow?"

"Not until noon tomorrow. Okay, we'll let them sleep and we can go over the café and listen to a cowboy band, maybe do some dancing."

After they left, Joanna said, "A classic care of avoiding a decision. She's asking herself, 'Do I like this guy enough to sleep with him?' She's had no one, now there are two handsome men immediately available." She chuckled and said, "It seems little Abby has not made up her mind yet. But that's their problem. I'm hoping my man comes back tonight."

"I'm going upstairs now."

"You better go pat your little maiden on her cute little butt if you want some attention tonight. I do believe she's a little peeved – I heard her throwing around dishes in the kitchen. I just hope they're my old cheap ones."

Luke went in the kitchen and hugged her warmly. She responded.

Joanna said, "You two go ahead. I'll finish up here."

The couple hugged and bounded up the stairs to Luke's room. They threw off their clothes and moved to the settee. Their lighthearted kisses turned to gentle caresses and then to devouring one another with mouths. She whispered to Luke, "I'm so wet. I can't last much longer."

"You take the lead"

"I will, you know. About time that the ladies were in charge."

"Nothing stopping you."

She moved over and straddled him athwart. His rigidity established her center and equilibrium, and she wildly moved up and down. Aroused and somewhat amused, Luke locked his arms behind his head and let her ride him. Her intensity grew, she moaned but never missed a stroke, and then came again.

She was sweaty and her eyes were glazed. He stood her up, walked her to the dressing mirror, leaned her forward and entered her from behind. He said, "I want to watch your face in the mirror, see how beautiful you are, and I want you to watch me when I hit my release."

After his climax, they rolled onto the floor rug and hugged side by side. She said, "Hold me tight, Luke." Her breathing relaxed. He softly kissed her forehead, and she said, "Hold me close. There'll be more loving before morning."

They stood up and rolled into their toasty bed, and into the post-coitus dimension that only sincere lovers know about.

About midnight, Luke heard the kitchen door open. Perro growled a bit but saw who the person was and went back to sleep. Luke and Alyce lay in bed, trying to stop giggling, as the mysterious person went quietly up the stairs to Joanna's room.

Alyce looked at her watch in the candlelight and said, "I give it about seven to eight minutes."

Luke massaged her back and buttocks as she checked her watch. As the minute hand hit eight, the bedsprings started creaking and soft moans of happiness drifted through the walls.

All was well in the boarding house. Doc was home.

Alyce whispered to Luke, "Again?"

"Sure thing, Lusty Lady. We did miss out for almost three days. We must catch up! We deserve the ecstasy."

Diez

Alyce was up early next morning and went downstairs to prepare breakfast with Joanna who seemed to be sleeping a little late. Luke could hear Doc still sawing logs in Joanna's room.

As Luke came down the stairs, Gregorio walked in for breakfast. Alyce set them out a coffee pot and two cups. Luke did the pouring and Gregorio said, "I need that. Abby kept me all night."

Luke laughed and said, "Good for you. I knew it would work between you two."

"Not what you're thinking. She's a talker, that one. She's kind of religious and spiritual, and believes God is a woman. I wrote down some of her words after I finally walked her home about midnight but didn't get an invite inside. I got a sisterly good night kiss and walked over to Doc's for a few hours sleep."

"Okay, what are the words? I'm curious as hell. I've heard other women mention that God is a female."

Gregorio took out a scribbled note, and he read, "We are women in God's human image. With the hot blood of our wombs we give form to new life; with the milk of our breasts, we suckle the children; and with nectar between our thighs we invite a lover, and then we birth a child; with our warm body we remind the world of its pleasures and sensation."

"Hot damn, can't argue with that. I especially like the 'nectar' part. That beautiful piece of anatomy is definitely sweeter than honey."

"It doesn't appear that she's about ready to share her nectar. I'm not feeling the attraction and energy."

"Maybe she just needs some time. Maybe the last man turned her off to the male gender."

"I'm thinking it's a one-sided attraction. I really like her but she's not showing any special interest in me. Maybe she wants you."

"Ain't going to happen. I'm totally happy with my little maiden." Alyce was listening on the other side of the door and heard every word. She smiled, and took the cinnamon rolls out of the oven. Joanna was working away by this time, cooking up some eggs and fresh ham. Alyce was humming an ancient love song.

The lingerie salesman, Rafael, strolled in for breakfast, looking like he'd been on a two-week drunk. His hair was amiss, and his suit was stained with everything from red wine to spaghetti sauce. His sample bag looked flat and empty.

Rafael said, "Coffee, please. I need coffee and keep it coming. It's gotta be hot and black."

Joanna noticed his empty bag and said, "Looks like you've been busy. Get money or stock-in-trade?"

"I'm not sure." He ate a quick breakfast and headed for a long siesta in his room.

Joanna chuckled and said, "He paid his rent for a whole week but I think he's only been here for a day or two."

Luke smiled and said, "With what's been going on here, he'd probably be complaining about all the noise at night. He might wanna bring back one of his wenches."

"Nope, not going to happen. No soiled doves in my boarding house."

Gregorio said, "Doc and all the guys will be over about ten this morning. We can get together and decide what we're going to about Leighton and the damn rustlers."

"Good, I've got a plan."

Tomas managed to make it over in an improvised wheelchair some would call a wheelbarrow. Freddy was walking under his own power with only the slightest limp. His eyes looked clear from a good night's sleep.

"Fellow travelers, here's my plan. I never really wanted to be a rancher - I'm a peace officer by trade. However, I am willing to give it a try. My father would want me to. I know we have to deal with Leighton and a few pesky Indians; and bad weather, droughts, market fluctuations, etc. But…"

Luke continued, "There's plenty of land for all us. Doc doesn't wanna be a rancher either but he would like a few steaks now and then, and maybe keep Joanna's boarding house supplied with meat. But for the rest of us, I am suggesting that we divide the land up as follows, and only if you want it: I'll keep the ranch house and cabin, or whatever are left of the buildings, and fifty square miles on the east. I want Carmen, Gregorio and Freddy to have twenty-five square miles on the southwest end, and the remaining twenty-five square miles to be divided between Carlos, Tomas, Hussong and Gabe. The line shacks could be the center of operations for the donated land."

Peripherally, Luke noticed that Rafael had casually walked back into the living room and was fiddling with the coffee pot. He didn't say a word or look up.

There was roar of approval about the land division as everyone shook hands back and forth. Luke added, "We can survey and mark the boundaries so there no's disagreement about who owns a certain mountain peak or who the creeks belong to. But everyone will be entitled to water and graze. Probably the best way to do that would to create a legal conglomerate, like a cattleman's association, but I'll leave that to you to decide; and how the costs and profits will be shared."

"Everyone has been helpful and kind to me, and there's way too much land for any one person. He looked at Carmen and asked, "Can you stay and work the land? My father would want you to stay, but I also know you want to return to Mexico."

Gregorio said, "Mama, maybe we can bring your relatives and friends to our land, rather than you going home."

"Or I go to Mexico sometimes like I did with Jesse. I would like to stay on the land. I love the freedom and the changing seasons."

"If we're all in agreement, then we'll go to Lawyer Dillard and prepare the deeds. I want them entered in the courthouse before we decide to take on Leighton and his band of ruffians. You should keep in mind that there may be gun battles and some of us could get hurt. I don't believe the Indians will be major problem – they'll either get back on the reservation and/or we can give them an occasional cow for food, like my father did."

"And fellow ranchers, start figuring out your ranch names and brands. That will look good on the deeds and make it more legal."

Gregorio took Luke aside and shook his hand, and expressed his thanks for supporting Carmen and her family.

Luke smiled and said, "My father would want it that way. He really loved Carmen. Now, here's a little news for you. I checked the property maps. Abby's stageline goes through the southwest corner of your land. Maybe she needs to talk to you about an easement –maybe a special deal could be worked out."

"I like it, Amigo. Sounds like a plan to get her to the bargaining table." He paused and added, "But there's something else we need to talk about."

"Let's palaver. What would that be?"

Carlos and Tomas had come to Luke about Gabe. They were happy about Hussong being a partner, but Gabe was another matter. Carlos said, "Gabe has a bad reputation for being obnoxious and profane to the extreme, especially after he's been drinking. He tends to gamble excessively and womanize often and spends any money he gets on his vices. That's some of the reasons that your father kept him out at a line shack and away from town and temptation. His health is shot too, smoking too many cheap cigars and chewing endless plugs of tobacco."

"What do you suggest?"

"We'll have to get tight controls of him with Lawyer Dillard, so he doesn't spend all the ranch's profits or get everyone tied in court litigation."

Luke concluded, "I'll work with Lawyer Dillard on the situation – get his ideas. I'll also talk to Gabe on the side. I like the old buzzard but he could cause a lot of trouble for everyone. I can see he's a basically good hand if he stays away from the whiskey."

Along with homemade brandy, Joanna and Alyce served refreshments of fresh cakes and cookies. In passing, Alyce caressed Luke on the shoulder, and he savored the largest, biggest smile that he had ever received from any female. This was going to be another good day.

Gregorio and Carlos proposed toasts to their new venture. It was a joyous time.

Luke was hoping that these good feelings and thoughts would last. Satan and his spawn were probably organizing in Phoenix for their next assault on the 3Q.

As the members of the group departed, a tow-headed boy came running up with a note and asked for "Gregorio Isaacs." Gregorio took the note and smiled. He gave the lad a nickel for his time.

Luke asked, "What is it? Enough of the suspense. What does the note say?"

"It's from Abby. I'm invited to her house for dinner after the afternoon stage run."

"You better take some massage oil. Her butt is going to be weary after that bumping along the trail."

"You're a bad man!" He left skipping down the sidewalk.

Alyce was standing just around the corner, and slyly asked, "Are you a bad man? Should I be frightened?"

"For the next two hours, you better be frightened, Little Maiden."

Once [1]

In the evening, the group met again at Joanna's to study the maps after the evening meal. The two groups had already worked out the names of their spreads and their brands. Because of the unexpected serendipity, the combined new owners of the ranches appeared to be compatible and willing to work together. Luke thought to himself, "I hope this harmony lasts. This is just too good to be true. If this mixed group of people can get along, maybe they could teach something to warring nations."

Luke noticed that Rafael had come downstairs and was sitting quietly in the far corner of the living room. He was trying to be inconspicuous by reading the latest *"Territorial Enterprise,"* which covered the news in Arizona and much of New Mexico. But his eyes kept shifting, looking up and down, and he seemed overly attentive to the new ranchers and their comments. By past experiences, Luke knew that salesmen, politicians, and lawyers required close scrutiny at all times.

Gregorio, Carmen and Freddy decided on calling their spread *The Bienvenido Rancho* with the brand *3MA (Three Mexican Americans)*;

Carlos, Tomas, Gabe and Hussong decided on their new ranch name *Good Fortune* with the brand *4LR (Four Lucky Ranchers)*. Luke was happy that they had set to work and were making plans.

Gabe and Carlos knew the layout of the ranch property better than anyone in town. Gabe had worked there for a dozen years, and Carlos had done odd jobs for Jesse and had guided bigwigs from back East on hunting expeditions on the ranch and to nearby mountains. Carmen knew both men and they had often stopped in for a meal at the main ranch house and to sleep in the bunkhouse. Jesse always looked forward to their visits to share a sip of whisky and several hours of male frontier braggadocio and belly-breaking laughter. He also enjoyed meeting the businessmen from back east and knowing they were probably successful in their enterprises but were definitely greenhorns and clumsy in the woods. Most of them had good senses of humor about their mistakes in the hills, like missing an easy shot because of "buck fever," or sliding down the side of a mountain through the mud, or accidentally misfiring their rifles and scaring the hell out of the pack animals…and the guides.

Gabe had arranged for a team of surveyors to go along with several of the men the next morning to lay out some rough boundaries. Luke wanted some basic drawings and ranch names entered into the court records before they made their next move. He fully planned on traveling to Phoenix and having a serious discussion with Timothy Leighton to advise him straight on that there was there was no chance of him taking over the 3Q lands. Luke knew the US Marshal based in Phoenix and planned on filling him in on Leighton's intentions. He also planned on taking along the reports from the local sheriff about the dead outlaws on his land.

Gabe took along Hussong and Carlos to watch his back and to help the surveyors when there were long distance sightings to measure on their gauges. Still on the mend, Tomas and Freddy stayed back. Carmen was safely and happily living with Doc's friend. The ladies were soon busy baking pies and sewing new dresses, and visiting with Joanna Carson for the neighborhood rumors and tales of questionable veracity.

Justifiably so, Gregorio stayed in Tucson and worked alongside Luke with the lawyers and getting the papers drawn up, and transferring ownership of the land to the new parties. Jesse had left a non-challenged will giving all the land to Luke, with a proviso by Carmen that she wouldn't challenge the will. Jesse had left her a sizeable bank account that would ensure that she was well taken care of for her remaining years. Now, she also had a third of the twenty-five square miles on the southwest scorner of the 3Q.

But Gregorio also had other plans for staying in town besides the legal papers. He wanted to find out once and for all if there was a chance with Abby. Their dinner the night before was comfortable and nice, and the conversation lively, but she didn't respond to any of his flirting or make any moves of seduction on her own. The night ended with a sisterly kiss… again.

He had enjoyed a number of women in his life – he had almost married several of them but at the last minute, he or she got cold feet about making their bond permanent. He knew about attraction and he felt it strongly with Abby. He was a practical man and rightfully assumed that if the woman wasn't interested, it was time to move on. He was not a stalker or a pleader, but a realist about the male-female relationship. He knew that frontier women did not want a sissy man, which was not his style by any means.

From what Luke had said, and how he viewed the relationship between him and Alyce, Luke was not interested in Abby. He seemed more than content with Alyce. Even though it was not fully accepted, he showed no concerns about a mixed racial marriage or what the mean gossips might say. There was also a twenty-year age difference but that didn't seem to be an issue for either of them. Luke said that Alyce would like to have another baby, and he was still capable. Time would tell the story on that one.

Luke had been married twice, and both women suffered from the continuing anxiety of him being injured or killed in law enforcement, and being away on manhunts weeks at a time. One wife just gave up and went home to her family in Oklahoma. She couldn't bear staying awake at night or jumping every time she heard a gunshot. They parted amicably but it took months for his heart to heal. The second wife, who seemed to be adjusting to his profession, succumbed to hepatitis after only two years of marriage. He had loved her completely, and her death set him back emotionally and he buried himself in his work. He took whatever investigations came his way and often volunteered for the real tricky, possibly lethal assignments.

There were no children from either marriage. His parents had died, he had no siblings, and he was pretty much alone on the earth. For the past ten years, he had enjoyed quick romances when they came along, and on long dry spells, enjoyed the attentions of the saloon ladies.

The little messenger boy showed up again with a note for Gregorio, just as they were entering the local restaurant. It was from Abby, asking if he wanted to take the afternoon mail run with her to Eloy. Her shotgun guard had called in sick. There was just one passenger who she would drop off at a nearby ranch. After delivering the mail, they could make a beeline back to Tucson and spend a relaxing evening together. Gregorio wrote "YEP" on the bottom of the note and gave the lad another nickel for taking the message back to Abby.

Gregorio looked at Luke, "Let's eat. I'm famished."

"You better build up your strength. They have huge steaks here. I think you'll need a lot of burning power tonight."

After lunch, Luke continuing working with the lawyer, while Gregorio helped Abby at the barn harnessing up the team. She was attentive and listening to every word from Gregorio. Within a half-hour, they were on the way to Eloy, a small mining settlement south of Phoenix.

Abby had unerring skill in keeping a jostling coach on track and applying the brakes as light as a feather and without a noticeable jar. Her five-foot-eight-inch frame handled the reins confidently and the mules responded accordingly, usually without her applying her black handmade whip. From saloon scuttlebutt, it was rumored that a drunken cowboy had tried to grab her one morning on the way to the stable, and she wrapped the whip around his ankles and he fell in the dirt and horse dung. She then whipped him on the ass and after he ran away, left town the next day from embarrassment.

Gregorio mentioned to Abby that he was impressed with her driving skills. She responded that she could sense the road's twists and turns by the sound of the stage's wheels, and by watching certain mules on the team.

She smiled and added, "I know I'm good. You just stay with your job – watch for those damn robbers."

The passenger was dropped off south of town at the "Crooked Spur Ranch." They hadn't seen any Indians or renegades and starting back, feeling that this was going to be a safe run. After watering the mules and bouncing along the road to Tucson, a masked lone rider suddenly appeared and ordered them to stop as they slowly climbed a sharp incline. He was an amateur and a fool, and had no idea that he was dealing with an experienced hand like Gregorio. He just saw what he perceived to be a weak woman and "some Mexican guy."

Through experience, Gregorio knew that you couldn't give any quarter to a masked outlaw, and he simply raised his scattergun from his lap, and shot the outlaw full center in the chest. The outlaw's last words were, "Holy shit, you shot me!"

Abby said about the same thing, "You plugged him dead center. That was so fast!"

As Gregorio looked around for other outlaws, he asked, "Should we have stopped and discussed the healthy value of Asian tea, or maybe the price of gold in New York City?"

She brought the coach to a complete stop and locked the reins around the brake handle. "No, you're right. You got him before he could shoot us. Let's go see who this gunsel might be."

The outlaw was definitely dead. The blow flies were already forming around his mouth and nose. She took off his bandana and saw that the outlaw was probably about 17 years old. Gregorio checked his horse and saddlebags.

She said, "Maybe he was just hungry, and needed money to eat."

"Not so. He's got three hundred bucks in his saddlebag, and plenty of rings and watches. His horse and saddle are good quality and his revolver and rifle are worth a hundred bucks. His saddle is even custom engraved with the name 'Jimmy' and a lot of carved designs and flairs."

Abby sighed, "It's too damn bad. Such a youngster."

"This stupid youngster has been busy. Luckily he didn't shoot us and maybe he's shot a few innocent folks. The sheriff might know."

Gregorio continued, "There's some soft sand over yonder. We'll throw him a shallow grave and make a report to the sheriff. The kid's got no identification. I haven't seen him on any wanted posters. My pals will want his horse and saddle, maybe his guns, and we'll take everything else down to the priest. He can use the money to buy food for his parishioners."

After they finished digging the grave with the coach shovel, Abby moved the Concord up to a green valley with a gentle stream. She set the brakes, let the horses stand in the stream and soak up the cooling waters. Gregorio and Abby were both hot and sweaty. She was the one that suggested that they strip down and take a plunge in a pool just a few yards upstream from the coach.

Gregorio asked, "Together? Right now?"

Matter-of-factly, she answered, "This is about the most privacy we'll have on our trip. Can you think of a better time or place?" Gregorio realized that Abby had made up her mind about their intimacy.

"Then we should make the best of it." They stripped slowly, watching one another. He enjoyed her pert breasts, her white creamy skin of her belly. He moved lower and appreciated her sweet aroma. She was a true blonde. They kissed with swirling tongues and open lips, again and again. Every time he touched and massaged her nipples, she shuddered and gasped. She reached down and began exploring his growing phallus. She dropped to her knees and kissed his manhood while slowly massaging his stones.

She looked upward and whispered, "It's been a long time for me."

"Wanna stop?"

"No damn way, *mi Corazon*. I've wanted you ever since I saw you the first time." As she walked to the coach to retrieve a blanket for the ground, he remembered wanting her when he saw her the first time in her tight jeans. She gave her naked backside an extra swing to each side. She smiled over her shoulder.

He entered her and within minutes, they had found love's ultimate peak. They rested a short while, and he filled her once again. She moaned with his delightful largeness and murmured, "I'm a daughter of Venus. I love it."

Gregorio chuckled to himself. It seemed that his little Abby had been reading the Greek classics, at least the ones with Aphrodite and her many suitors, or maybe about the ruins of Pompeii where even the emperor's wife went at nighttime for her daily dose of love-making.

They lay back on the blanket and watched the big white fluffy clouds in the bright blue sky. Insects were chirping away, and they saw a big buck across the stream come down for a drink.

Abby asked, "Can we stay here forever? This must be what heaven is like."

"There's plenty more love and pleasure waiting for us in Tucson. Right now, we have to get moving before its dark. In a few more hours, the mountain lions and bears will be down for a drink and they might decide two naked humans would be tasty."

"I like being naked with my man."

"You'll never know how happy I am to hear that. You were so hesitant and I wasn't looking for a sister."

They started to dress. "I wasn't completely sure about you until I saw you take on that outlaw. I like your *machismo* and your fast thinking."

"Just taking care of my lady in distress."

"And you did well, my knight. Let's get to town. Maybe I'll see you later this evening?"

"Wild horses and bands of well-armed ruffians couldn't keep me away."

As they rolled into town, Gregorio saw Rafael leaving the telegraph office. When their eyes met, Rafael looked away. He didn't give it too much thought, figuring Rafael maybe had bad eyes and couldn't see him, or was ordering some new stock from his home office for the ladies.

He nudged Abby and asked, "Would you like a new silky nightgown?"

"Whatever for, my sire? I won't be needing night gowns any more."

Doce

Timothy Leighton's large suite was on the third floor of the Emporium Building in downtown Phoenix. The building was only several blocks away from the government headquarters of the Arizona Territory; and housed several upscale restaurants, beauty parlors, and clothing shops. It also had several doctor and dentists offices, with a sign that said, "All University Trained." It was a busy center during the daytime.

Even though early in the morning, Leighton had his feet up on his desk and was sipping a brandy and smoking a long stogie. He liked to look out his large bay window and fantasize about taking over the entire territory and becoming the next governor. He already had a dozen legislators and judges bought and paid for. Some he ensured their cooperation with money and land, and others he got them cheating on their taxes or wrangling insurance frauds, or playing with young underage girls in his brothels. Local law enforcement was a joke – the sheriff and town marshal were corrupt and incompetent. They had no training and didn't know the difference between a felony or tort. The US Marshal was a political crony who was always worried about being re-appointed in every federal administration, so therefore did nothing to upset anyone. The marshal had several hard-working deputies that he figured eventually he would have to discredit them with false revelations that they were abusing whiskey and drugs or tapping their tools on young boys, or just send them to Boot Hill.

The governor of Arizona was completely under his influence. Leighton' sister Judith was strong-willed with a cold, pragmatic heart. Leighton had arranged for the lily-livered governor to meet and marry Judith. The rest was easy. He did whatever he was told by Judith, and if he was cooperative, she would occasionally take him to her bedroom.

Leighton was also working at bringing New Mexico under his control and had already established an office in Albuquerque. The governor in that territory was just too easy to control – he was a drunk and a compulsive gambler.

Leighton found that if persuasion and blackmail didn't work, he had a gang of goons that would do whatever was necessary to make the citizenry cooperative. Their specialties were beatings, house and business burnings, seizures of bank accounts, and rapes of womenfolk in front of their fathers or husbands. Law enforcement was blind to the law violations and often they participated in some of the illegal acts in chasing certain people out of Arizona. It was reported that Leighton actually had opponents "tarred and feathered" and run out of town "on a rail."

Treated even with less respect were the former slaves, Hispanics, Indians, Asians and females. Leighton considered them definitely the weaker sex intended merely for cooking and house cleaning, and of course, sex on demand.

A knock on the door broke his reverie. His clerk Benjamin entered and said, "Sorry to bother you Mr. Leighton, but I just received a telegram from our man in Tucson."

"What does he want? More money?"

"No, sir. He has some important news. Remember the 3Q ranch, and we thought it would be easy pickings? Well, Rafael tells us that the son has returned and is taking over the ranch. He's already doing land surveys and title searches, and has split the land between his friends and relatives. They plan on working it."

"How the hell can they? We've stolen most of their cows – even took their prize bulls." He paused, "And what about all the yahoos we sent up there to scare the cowboys and burn the buildings?"

Benjamin, knowing his boss's wrath, cast his eyes to the floor, and said, "They're all dead. The son, Luke Quinn, is a former US Marshal and a strong fighter."

Leighton slammed his cigar and glass to the floor, and complained, "What the hell! I can't even get efficient hired killers."

"I'll tell the sheriff. Maybe he knows some more gunslingers. Should be a few stashed in prison that we can spring for the 3Q job."

"Good, and get 'em to Tucson. I want all those cowboys taken out for good, everyone associated with the land."

"How about the old wife?"

"Yeah, her too. Get 'em all."

Benjamin suggested, "Maybe you might want to wait for a week or so. Rafael tells us that Luke Quinn is coming to Phoenix to talk to you direct."

"Maybe that could work. We'll just ambush them on the road, or get them into jail on a trumped-up charge, and hang them from the ancient oak in the courtyard."

"It could work."

"Do we still have that sneaky little bastard, Billy, and his loco brother working for us? They're always ready for bushwhacking and nasty assignments. Billy is a sick lunatic. I still can't understand how he can have sex with an unwilling female in front of her family, and with his fellow gunsels watching. He's definitely a mental case that one. Let me know if he ever starts turning on us – we'll have to drop him down the Grand Canyon some night."

"Yeah, he's around. But he gives me the creeps. He personifies evil. He has no human values, animal feral." Benjamin added, "Animals usually kill for a reason, like territory or food; but Billy kills and hurts just for the fun of it. He told his pals that killing is better than sex."

"Have him come see me, but I want two of my bodyguards here during the meeting – and take away his guns, including the knife in his boot, before he comes into the office."

"Done, I'll send Harry and Gib to find him, maybe later this afternoon."

Leighton went back to daydreaming. For him, the 3Q situation was a minor setback. He had the means and yahoos to take care of the problem.

The thoughts of more land began to excite him, deep down in his innards. He rang a bell for Benjamin.

"I want that little honey-blonde from Vicky's crib, the little farm-girl that ran away from Iowa. I think it's time I did an in-depth report for my friends who have been waiting for the go-ahead."

"Will she be staying for lunch?

"No, I'll be putting her back to work afterwards."

"Okay, lunch at one o'clock. I've talked to Harry and Gib. They'll bring Billy over at three."

Trece

A week passed. All the romances continued. If it wasn't for the stagecoach schedule, or Gregorio needing to see the lawyer about the land contracts, Abby and Gregory had pretty much dropped out of sight. Neighbor children often came home giggling and telling their parents that funny noises were coming out of Abby's house.

The surveyors came in from the land. They had one minor skirmish with three braves but after a few shots were fired, the Indians decided to vamoose northerly which took them off of 3Q land. Very few cattle had been spotted anywhere on the land. Carmen's cabin and Gabe's line shack were still both standing. The men stayed in those buildings several times but Bob's cabin had been burned to the ground. There was still no sign of Bob.

Carmen asserted, "That Bob was always untrustworthy. Jesse should have fired him. I'd bet he threw in with the outlaws.

Gregorio said, "If that's the case, he's probably dead. Even criminals don't trust turncoats. If they'll turn on someone they're working for, they'll turn on you too. Once they're no longer needed, off they go to some unmarked grave. Even desperadoes know that."

The meeting this evening included Tomas and Freddy. They were young and healthy, and were close to being healed. They were all ears, still doubting their good fortune, being young men and already owning property.

Luke said, "We have the contracts finished and ready for signature, two copies of each, one for each person and the other for legal records. Doc will witness each document. Everything is as we discussed. Once signed, we'll take everything over to the courthouse and get the papers officially registered. The survey reports will be attached."

Gregorio added, "Times may get tough in the next few months. Leighton may well send more outlaws out our way. That's his style. He threatens and scares people. So if something deadly happens, you have to be ready to assign your percentage of the land to a beneficiary. That too will stop a lot of court action. When you have this many people involved, you have to have a clear line of inheritance. One piece of land can jeopardize the whole operation and everybody else."

Meanwhile, Rafael had quietly drifted into the back of the room. He was obviously listening to every word. After the meeting adjourned, Luke gestured to Gregorio and said that they needed to have a little talk with Rafael about his interest in their land. They walked over and took him by the arm and walked him outside.

Luke started, "Okay, Rafael. What the hell is going on? You listen to every word and you have no business with us, except selling pantaloons and nighties. Gregorio and Abby spotted you at the telegraph office, and Joanna's friend works there. She said that you have been sending telegrams almost every other day."

Rafael quivered and looked in every direction except at them He was already shaking – his eyes started blinking uncontrollably. Luke knew this little rat would be easy to question. He had seen it before. Rafael was up to something and men like him like to work in the shadows.

Rafael sniveled in a high voice, "Nothing. I'm not doing anything except checking with my home office. The ladies at the Painted House bought all my stock. Sure, I had sex with them but that's not your concern. That's my business. I just have to figure out a way to disguise the loss of profit to my boss in Omaha."

Gregorio continued, "But why the interest in our land dealings? What's that all about?"

"I don't know anything. I'm not doing anything to you men."

Gregorio said to Luke, "You believe this jerk?? Or should I just take him out back and beat the living daylights out until he tells the truth?"

"You might hurt your knuckles. He's not worth it!"

"We know he's a lying little jerk. What do you wanna do with him? He knows what going on, and we might as well find out now… before we ride in for a talk with Leighton."

Luke smiled and said, "Every time he walks past Perro, my little buddy snarls and growls, and barely lets him go by. Perro is an excellent judge of character. He doesn't like this spy at all."

"What do you suggest?"

"I say take this piece of garbage out in the backyard, tie him to a tree, and let Perro have a go at him."

Rafael started to shake even more. Tears began swelling up in his eyes. "You guys can't do that to me. The other people will hear, and they'll summon the sheriff. He'll arrest you guys for assault and battery."

Luke said, "If you've been informing to Leighton, he knows our plans and those people in the living room might get hurt or shot. You really think they'll care if you are "accidentally" attacked by dog?"

"You're bluffing. You won't do it." Rafael's voice now became low and husky. His threat was dry and constricted and his breathing labored.

Gregorio took him by the arm and walked him outside to the tree. Luke grabbed a rope from the back porch, and tied him to the trunk, his arms behind his back. Perro had joined them and was jumping and barking, as were Joanna's two dogs. The dogs didn't quite know the plan but they were willing join in on the fun. Gregorio and Luke put them on leashes.

Rafael insisted, "I don't know anything." The barking grew louder.

Luke released Perro with an attack command. Perro tore into the jerk by grabbing him by the right leg and trying to pull him down to the ground, but the rope kept Rafael in a standing position. Spotting of blood appeared on his trousers. Luke hooked Perro back up on his leash, and released Joanna's pet dogs. They were basically pets and just ran around Rafael, sniffing him and taking playful tugs at his trousers. They licked the blood on his right leg.

Luke declared, "Here it comes, Rafael. Another attack from Perro, and this time he will go for your gonads. Once the other dogs see this and smell your fear, the pack mentality will take over and you will just a piece of meat for three growling, howling mutts. Your call?"

Luke reached for the leash and collar holding Perro. Rafael's eyes widened, and he yelled, "No, don't do it. I'm begging you. For the Holy Mother of Creation, don't do it. I'll tell you the whole story."

Gregorio said, "Glad to hear it. Perro will be at your heel the whole time. You best be honest. You can see he's probably feeling cheated for not having a meal of mountain oysters."

Joe Race

"Just the honest truth. If you mess with us, we'll just mention to Leighton how you squealed and gave us his whole operation."

"No, don't do that. Gawd no, he'll kill me."

Luke untied him and walked him over to as picnic table. He slapped Rafael several times, and asserted, "Now, the truth. I don't want our people getting hurt."

Rafael laid out the whole operation and Leighton's future plans. Leighton said that he had heard Luke was coming from Denver and had plans for the 3Q. He telegraphed Rafael in Denver who decided to ride along on the stages and find out what he could. It worked out perfectly when he met Luke on the stagecoach with the Abby woman. He said that he tried to make it with her, and had no luck. Rafael added, "She must be a lesbian." Gregorio slapped him on the back of the head.

Rafael said, "What the hell?"

Luke ordered, "Keep talking."

"Once I found the information out from the boarding house discussions, I just kept sending the details to Leighton. I worked for him before in several other land claims."

Gregorio asked, "Were people ever killed from what you told Leighton?"

Rafael cast his eyes to the ground. "I don't know. Some of them were run off their ranches. I just do my informing but never do any of the dirty work. He's got large numbers of people willing to work for him. They come from everywhere, drifters mainly, or gunslicks that worked in other gangs. They're a deadly bunch of bastards. I always tried to stay away from them." He added, "He wants the 3Q which is in the center of his other lands. He wants to complete the land puzzle. He didn't go after your father because he was ready to die. He just figured the old Mexican wife would just go back to Mexico. He didn't plan on you showing up, or Gregorio, the son of the old lady."

He reluctantly continued, "And he didn't plan on having so many new landowners in on the deal."

"Does he send messages back to you?"

"Yeah, he has an erratic code system." Luke asked, "Does he know we're coming?"

"He knows, and has several ambushes planned for your group. He also has some wild gunsel named Billy Jones, ready to call you out for a gunfight, or to backshoot you right in downtown Phoenix. Billy's younger brother, Jimmy, is just as crazy but he hardly knows which end of the barrel the bullet comes out."

Luke looked at Gregorio and asked, "Do you suppose?"

"Is Billy a scrawny kid with weird eyes?"

"That's him. Even the other outlaws fear this guy, because he's so unpredictable. He loves violence. He likes to hurt people. I met him one time on another job. He broke a leg on a *viejo* just because the old man was slow to answer."

Gregorio had already told the story to Luke about the outlaw who had tried to rob the stagecoach driven by Abby. Apparently Jimmy was not going to be a problem.

"Do you know anything about a wrangler named Bob who used to work the 3Q?"

"I didn't know him face to face, but I was told that he was informing about the 3Q to Leighton. That's how the boss knew about the condition of old Jesse and that you were coming?"

Gregorio said, "We couldn't find him out at the line shack. Did he get paid off or run away?"

"No, nothing like that. Billy found out that Bob had been saving his money. Billy asked him out outside of the shack on the pretext of having a drink at sunset and then cold-as-can-be, shot him in the back. His body is supposedly on the bottom of a cliff near the line shack.   Billy just left him out there for the wolves and cougars."

"How about Monte, another drover at one of the line shacks?"

Rafael answered, "I don't know Monte, but he might have been the guy who saw Billy and the other outlaws coming up a valley trail. I guess he took off – it was reported to Leighton that one of the line shacks cowboys took off on a fast-moving horse, and never looked back."

Luke said, "Now, what do we do with you? We let Billy get away one time and now we have to fight that stupid son-of-a-bitch again."

Gregorio said, "Let's just kill him and dump him in the desert. The cougars can take care of him – no more informing and no body."

"Or give him to Perro and the other dogs. They're hungry."

"I won't talk. I promise." He started crying again.

Luke said, "We've heard that bullshit before. We gotta keep you incommunicado – away from stagecoaches and telegraph offices."

A voice from the shadows said, "I can take him to my Navajo village. My family will keep him there as long as you want. If he tries to escape, they will fill his back with arrows." Alyce stepped forward. "Even if he managed to escape, there are hundreds of miles of red rock bluffs and dozens of dead-end canyons."

Luke smiled and said, "That sounds like a plan. We'll take him out to the village tomorrow and introduce him to the elders. We'll send along some food and gifts."

"How long do you want him there?"

"Maybe two to three weeks, and then they can release him. Keep him for a month to be safe. Put him on a train to Denver. The tribe can keep all his possessions except for his clothes and I'll give him a five dollar gold piece for his travel."

Gregorio asked, "And for tonight?"

Alyce said, "We'll keep him tied up in the pantry. Perro can guard the door. If he tries to escape, it'll be a bloody mess." She continued, "I'll ask Mrs. Carson to see her telegraph friend, and make sure that no messages are sent to anyone about this whole situation."

Rafael asked, "How about my wounded leg. Your damn dog bit me."

Gregorios slapped him again on the back of the head. "You insult Abby and now you're cussing out Luke's dog. You've got no manners."

"Sorry. Will you please find me the doctor?" Rafael sunk lower in his chair.

Gregorio said, "That's more like it. We'll get Doc for you. He might still be in the living room."

Luke told Perro to watch over Rafael. He wagged his tail and sat right in front of the frightened informant. The other mutts didn't know what the orders were, but they sat next to Perro, also wagging their tails.

Doc and the land group were still jawing in the living room. Luke explained what had transpired with Rafael and what the plans were for riding to Phoenix. He said that he, Gregorio, Alyce and Abby would go to the southern end of the Navajo Indian Reservation with Rafael. He told the group to be ready to ride to Phoenix in about three days. Tomas and Freddy were adamant that they wanted to go. Luke said, "Up to Doc."

Gregorio then remembered, "Doc, we've got a dog bite victim for you to look at. No hurry."

Doc said, "That's good. Joanna is bringing out fresh apple pies with whipped cream on top." He chuckled and added, "She even got some ice out of the storage shed and made vanilla ice cream."

Alyce said, "I'll make some fresh coffee."

Catorce

The men left for Phoenix the next day as a group with plans to camp along the way for several days. Gabe was hung-over and looked sick. Tomas and Freddy were in good shape and as young men, were ready for whatever came their way.

Abby had provided the men with the names of four inconspicuous hotels about a mile from the capitol buildings. On the fourth day, the group would rendezvous at the Mojave Hotel to finalize their plans for approaching Leighton. The men wore standard cowboy clothing with nothing remarkable or noticeable that would garner the attention of the hardcases.

Unknown to the men, the ladies also had plans. On the day after the men left, Abby hitched up her stagecoach and made ready for the trip to Phoenix. Far ahead of the social times, the ladies had made personalized male jeans for a tight, comfortable fit and sewed various colors of calico shirts, and made ready to help Luke and Gegorio in Phoenix. To conceal any suspicion of their "manhood," the women made the shirts with box pleats to conceal their bosoms. The women wore their hair up inside their dusty cowboy hats and for anyone looking at them from afar, they would appear to be western men taking a ride to the big city. They were well-armed. Carmen had her scattergun, and Joanna favored a lever-action Winchester carbine rifle. Abby and Alyce each wore gun belts with Colt .44's. They had plenty of ammunition and stopped along the way several times for practice and fired off dozens of rounds.

Abby handled the reins, while Alyce rode shotgun. They both carried hidden .41 caliber derringers in the small pocket designed for round watches.

Abby said, "I pity the outlaws that try to hold us up on this trip. The adrenaline is running high."

Alyce smiled, "I hope it happens. We need the shooting practice."

"You sound anxious to fight and are about as deadly as a rattler. Hope the men appreciate us showing up."

"It'll be a surprise for sure. As long as we don't become like weepy pansies and a burden, we'll do okay. Our men want us to be strong."

"Well, some men would us to stay home, do housework and have babies. But I think you're right about Gregorio and Luke. They want equal partners, not some weepy, complaining female."

Abby asked, "Alyce, what is your background anyway? You don't seem like a meek little gal from an Indian tribe. You're more than a simple maid."

"I am definitely an Indian and very proud to be. I work for Joanna while things are calming down on the Reservation. After my graduation at the Indian school, I helped the soldiers with several investigations, and they taught me how to shoot. I worked a case where a huge, ugly Indian was going berserk with sexual crimes. He was from another tribe, and no one knew him or could identify him. With my approval, the soldiers set me up as a decoy in a remote hut in the foothills, and he came in one night, and tried to rape and kill me." She patted her derringer, but he didn't expect an armed female who was willing to fight." She paused, "By the time my soldier backup got into my hut, I had already shot him and finished him with my Bowie knife. He would never harm another female."

Abby inquired, "There were other incidents?"

"Sure, I worked undercover on several theft cases. One of the cases showed that the Indian Agent was not sending the right number of cattle to the Reservation or he was sending sick, skinny stock. And you'll never guess who the agent worked for?"

"Sounds like it could be a Leighton operation."

"You got it. As soon as I heard about the big outlaw boss trying to take over the 3Q, I knew it had to be Leighton. So, in reality, I'm working with Luke and also for the Bureau of Indian Affairs. Washington, D.C. wants our tribes to be treated fairly. That's probably one of the reasons that the San Carlos Apaches have jumped the Reservation. They're tired of being lied to or cheated on the promised supplies."

"Well, maybe we can even some scores. Our men and their compadres are willing to fight, and no one fights fiercer than a man or woman fighting for their own land and family."

Alyce reminiscenced, "And that's why the Indian Wars are taking so long to finish. Our people are fighting for what they perceive as rightfully theirs. Hopefully a compromise can be worked out. The people fleeing from Europe to the USA are without end. I'm afraid that our people will perish if they don't find a compromise with honor."

The travel days passed quickly and the tension among the landowners increased as they knew the time was coming for a showdown with Leighton's ruffians. The men got to their hotels without incident, but they were totally set back when they went to the Mojave Hotel for their planning session and found the four women already showered, sitting in the lobby sipping dark black Mexican coffee. The male duds had been put away. This time they were dressed as fashionable ladies of the time, full petticoats and modern hats with peacock feathers. There were hugs all around and excited greetings.

Gregorio looked at Abby and said,"I'm sure you have a good explanation for this, and Mother, how did you end up in this mess?"

Abby stepped forward and asserted, "Look, we're all in this together. We decided we would come to Phoenix and help any way possible. We're not helpless females and there are many ways we can help besides fighting and shooting."

Luke asked, "And what would this be?" He reached over and took Alyce's hand.

Alyce said, "We can walk around and just about go anywhere without raising suspicion. We make good spies – remember the ladies working both sides in the Civil War? I can't go into some of the white quarters because I'm an Indian and likely wouldn't be welcome. But then our white ladies can't go into the Mexican and Indian quarters and listen to the gossip. Some of the outlaws are mixed breeds, so that can be confusing."

Luke answered, "I think you're on to something. I hadn't quite figured out how I was going to approach Leighton without getting shot. Abby and Joanna could walk around and into Leighton's business building and get an idea of the layout, and how much security he has in place. Being well-dressed Caucasian women, you won't attract any attention. Carmen and Alyce, you could snoop around in the Mexican sections; maybe go to a beauty shop, and listen to the rumors. The men will just stay low and inconspicuous for the next day or two, until we get some information back."

Gregorio said, "I've arranged for a private room so we can plan, and also the staff is bringing…are you ready?… large plates of fresh seafood from the Gulf of Mexico. And of course, we'll have the refried *frijoles* and plenty of *rojo* rice. We're in the big city so we might as well enjoy all the culinary amenities."

The meal was scrumptious and the conversation jovial, especially after a dozen bottles of *vino* from Spain. A plan was made to re-meet in the same room on the next day at the same time. By that time, pieces of concrete information would be ready.

Gregorio left with Abby for her private room. Alyce gestured for Luke to follow her to her room on the second floor. The rest of the group stood, made their good-byes, and made plans to return to their respective hotels.

Luke had noticed that Gabe had been drinking heavily and wasn't intermingling with his fellow land owners. As he walked with Alyce to her room, he noticed that Gabe was entering a hotel carriage… alone.

Luke was considering that probably he should follow the old trailhand, until he felt a sight tug on his arm from the gorgeous Alyce.

"Come on Marshal. We have some serious catching-up to do. It's been almost four days. Much too long – you've spoiled me."

"Okay, if I must." She playfully punched him on the shoulder, and giggled.

At that very moment, he clearly knew he was falling completely in love. There was no sense in resisting.

He looked out the front window one more time and thought, "Gabe's on his own, drunk and stupid as he might be. That old codger walks around with a cloud over his head."

Quince'

If Gabe didn't have bad luck, he wouldn't have any luck at all. He was feeling left out at the meeting, and was realizing that he didn't want to be a landowner and rancher. He didn't want the responsibility of a 24-7 life, and especially managing employees and figuring the weight of cows for market on the ratio how much land and graze were available. He didn't see the donated land from Luke as a gift but rather a burden and restriction on his freedom and ability to move out whenever he wanted.

Gabe had enjoyed six strong drinks at the strategy meeting; but he wanted more. In his fuzzy brain, he assumed he could think clearer about the ranch if he just had a few more drinks. He asked the hotel driver to take him to a popular saloon where he might play some dice, find a woman and down a few more whiskeys. With his luck running from bad to worst, the driver took him to the Lucky Lady Saloon.

Gabe walked inside and the joint was to his liking. There was a noisy honky-tonk piano playing in the background, and like most saloons, he noticed there was stairway leading to the girls upstairs. Many of the girls were flittering about trying to snag a customer. They really looked good to him – he hadn't been with a woman for over two years,

His arthritic knees had been bothering him since they started the ride from Tucson to Phoenix, and his mental condition was making him feel depressed. He addled to a quiet corner of the bar, and ordered a double shot with a beer chaser. After the second round, he was started to feel almost normal. He was now about ready for the ladies.

A couple of boisterous cowboys took the seats near his quiet corner. They were loud and jostled one another, with one cowboy knocking over his beer. Gabe gave him his best warning look, and asked him to buy a replacement beer.

The rowdy cowboy was playing the fool and showing off for his friends. He just ignored Gabe and finally shouted, after Gabe asked him again for another beer, "Shuddup, old timer. Old farts like you should be home in bed with some feeble bitch under a patchwork quilt. This bar is for young people who want to drink and raise hell."

Gabe asked, "You wanna take it outside?" Gabe was a short, barrel-chested man who usually won his fights by coming up under his opponent's arms and driving his head into the solar plexus. Once the air was knocked out of his opponent, the fight was usually over. Gabe was figuring this yahoo was drunk and would be an easy target.

But he didn't figure on what happened next. One of the cowboy's friend said, "Hey, is that Joe's shirt and hat you're wearing? I was with him when he bought 'em at the general store. There weren't any other like that, matching colors and all, and they had just come in from New York."

Gabe answered, "I don't know anything about some Joe's clothes. These are mine...bought 'em myself in Tucson."

The friend said, "I know those are Joe's shirt and hat. Look inside the hat brim, Joe wrote his name. Joe and the guys went out to the 3Q a few weeks ago, and Joe never made it back."

The drunken cowboy reached out and knocked the hat off of Gabe's head. The friend looked inside the brim and saw Joe's name. Gabe could sense this was not going well, and he was outnumbered. All six of the cowboys were wearing pistols.

Gabe, thinking the best he could with his booze-addled brain, figured he would blast one of the cowboys and make a run for the batwings of the saloon. The other cowboys would be stunned and not react fast enough. Hopefully there would be a saddled horse at the hitching post and he could ride like hell out of the town and into the desert darkness. His bravado was spot on, but not supported in reality by too many whiskeys in his past, and a weary body with bad knees.

The cowboys were not expecting Gabe to be aggressive. Without hesitation, he drew his .45 caliber revolver and shot the first cowboy full in the chest. He managed to get off a second shot which caught the friend in the neck and took out his carotid artery. Those two were finished. As he ran, he tripped and fell over the first cowboy.

As he was limping to the batwings, he quickly glanced back to see who was pursuing him, maybe take another or two. Halfway down the stairs leading to the whore's cribs stood a man who looked vaguely familiar. He had his revolver pointed directly at Gabe's chest. Before Gabe could react, the cartridge exploded, and the bullet burned into his chest and he collapsed to the floor. The man from the stairs walked over and stood over Gabe. He now knew it was the freaking kid Billy Jones from the line shack.

Billy asked, "Remember me, you old bastard? You were going to hang me."

Gabe was a true westerner and wasn't about to ask for mercy or a doctor. He managed to utter, "Sorry we didn't complete the job."

Billy asked, "What are you in town for? Where are the rest of those 3Q wranglers?"

"Don't know what you're talking about. I quit a few days ago and I'm riding on to Los Angeles."

Billy stated, "One more time, you old coot. Why are you here?"

Gabe managed to raise the middle finger of his right hand and thrust it towards Billy. It was Gabe's last act of strength and courage.

Billy calmly shot him between the eyes, and said, "Crazy old bastard."

Billy looked across at the spectator cowboys and said, "You boys clean up this mess. And bartender, I want you to get some soap and wash down the floorboards. Fresh blood is not good for business."

Billy reached down and cleaned out Gabe's pockets. He only had a pocket knife, a few dollars, six extra bullets, and a hotel key without a name.

He gestured for Jake, one of the more intelligent outlaws in his gang, "Jake, I want you to get your ass moving and find out how Gabe got here…maybe a hotel cab, and find out what hotel he came from. There's something going on. Gabe wasn't about to quit his job and move to California. It would have been too tough for an old cowhand to start over without any money. His few dollars wouldn't have even got him out of Arizona."

Dieciseis

Next morning, Carlos, Tomas and Hussong assembled in the breakfast room of their hotel. They quickly ascertained that Gabe hadn't slept in his room. In a check with the front desk clerk, Hussong learned that Gabe hadn't come back to the hotel. The clerk checked his log and said that Gabe had been dropped off at the Lucky Lady Saloon by the hotel cab the evening before. The clerk added that the Lucky Lady was a notorious saloon for any type of criminal or lowlife. He said that saloon was not safe, even if cowboys travelled in pairs or groups. He added that he had heard that outlaws from all over the West came there to look for jobs, any kind of rustling, killing, robbing jobs. He chuckled and said, "It's like an employee clearing house for vicious criminals, sleaze balls and dipshits."

The men went about their breakfast. Hussong noticed that a scruffy cowboy had walked over to the front desk and was jabbering with the clerk. The cowboy reached in his pocket and grabbed several coins and passed them to the clerk. The cowboy and clerk then looked in the direction of the men at breakfast. When Hussong noticed this and their eyes locked, the cowboy quickly looked away.

Hussong said, "I've got go talk to that guy. He's probably paying for some information about us." Hussong rose and walked to the front desk area.

The scruffy cowboy saw him coming and ran to the front door. But Hussong was faster and caught him by the arm, and spun him around. He said, "I need to talk to you."

"I'm not talking to some dirty Indian. Let me go." He hit Hussong full in the face with a right cross, and Hussong fell to the floor. The cowboy started to draw his revolver, but before he could clear leather, Carlos shot him through the left ear. He died instantly, no twitching and almost no blood. No heartbeat left.

The desk clerk joined the group and said, "Now you've done it. That's one of Leighton's men. His name is Jake, kind of a low level arm breaker. Leighton's the kingpin in this town. Our hotel pays him fifty bucks a month for insurance —most businesses do it or else suddenly you have a mysterious fire, and the sheriff doesn't do anything. He's on Leighton's payroll."

Tomas inquired, "What was he asking about? Why did he give you money?"

"He mainly talked about Gabe, one of your partners. Jake said Gabe was killed last night in the saloon after he shot two cowboys. Jake wanted to know who Gabe was travelling with and why he was in town. I have no idea why you men are in town, but I did point you out to him. If I hadn't, he would have beaten the holy crap out of me, maybe rape my bookkeeper. Likely he wouldn't do it today but maybe some night he would send two miscreants and do us in. They're rotten, nasty human beings."

Tomas asked, "Were you going to tell us so we would be on alert?"

"Of course! I took his money, and let him think I was completely cooperative. We're all in this together against these outlaws."

Carlos asked, "What do you suggest we do now since the sheriff is corrupt?"

"I think you should skedaddle and head for the US Marshal's Office and make your report. Grab your gear and get out of the hotel. If you go the local sheriff, you'll find yourself in a jail cell and waiting for the hangman after a bullshit trial. He'll arrest the rest of you for accessories or some other phony charge."

"How about witnesses to self defense, protecting Hussong?"

"Do you see anyone left here in the lobby or restaurant? They're all gone and won't remember a thing. There's nobody for the sheriff to interview. No one cares about Indians anyway."

Hussong asked, "How about you? You saw him draw on me while I was down."

"As always, I'll be fat, dumb and happy... and alive! I won't remember a thing, nothing about Jake or you men. I'll just say I was in the back office doing paperwork, heard a shot, and then saw a dead body." He added, "By now, someone might have told the sheriff. So... get your gear and move on quickly."

Within minutes, the men were on the road and walking briskly to Luke and Gregorio's hotel. Carlos figured it would be smart to get off the street and have the US Marshal come to them, especially since Luke was a retired deputy. No one tried to stop them or say a word. It was generally taken as a means of survival not to hear or see anything, unless there might be money in it from Leighton. Back-stabbing informants are always a problem in any enterprise or community.

They found Luke and Gregorio and their ladies at breakfast. Carmen and Joanna were still at the rendezvous hotel, and about ready to meet with Abby and Alyce. The plans still had Carmen and Alyce checking out the Mexican and Indian areas, while Abby and Joanna were going to do a casual surveillance at Leighton's Emporium Building and environs. When Carlos and his partners neared the table, the two ladies were chattering about the day's events and excited about finding a good manicurist and maybe a massage parlor.

Luke was saying, "You ladies be careful around those massage parlors. I've heard those masseurs can find pleasure spots that none of us know about."

As she rose to leave, Alyce kissed Luke on the neck and said, "You've already taught me all about my little sensitive areas."

Abby smiled at Gregorio and said, "You too, hombre. No worries about our beauty and massage stops."

Carlos abruptly said, "We gotta talk and in private. Gabe's been murdered, and I just shot one of Leighton's men when he tried to kill Hussong."

Luke answered, "Shit, let's go to my room. Do you think the ladies will be safe?"

"Yeah, no problem there. Nothing to worry about with the ladies. Leighton doesn't know about them."

Abby said, "Then we'll run along and check back after lunch. We'll meet back at our Mojave Hotel and then have our strategy meeting in the afternoon."

Once inside the room, Carlos told Gregorio and Luke what he knew about Gabe getting himself killed; and how he shot one of Leighton's lieutenants, Jake. He said that the only people that knew about the 3Q operation in Phoenix maybe would be the two cowboys that Gabe shot, and Jake, who were all dead. He also mentioned that probably the desk clerk would not inform on them. But none of them knew that Billy Jones was the wild card in the deck. That deadly rattlesnake was still in the shadows.

Luke felt that Freddy would blend in nicely with the local populace while walking to the US Marshal's Office and asking the marshal to come to the hotel. He wrote a quick note, which said,

"Urgent. Please come promptly. Please be discreet. Need your help." He signed it Luke Quinn, retired Deputy Marshal, Denver office. On the bottom of the note, he added, "P.S. The bearer of this message, Freddy, can escort you to our hotel. He speaks good English."

Carlos asked, "What do you know about this lawman? Maybe I should jump on my horse and escape to Mexico."

"That's always an option. You could get to Mexico in two to three days if you rode hard, and then again, the telegraph is faster than your horse. Maybe the sheriff would notify his other rotten pals along the way." He smiled and asked, "And you would give up Miss Abby?"

Gregorio nodded negatively.

Luke continued, "Here's what I know about the local marshal. I already sent a telegram to Denver for a background check. Gus O'Reilly, the marshal, is an honest man and about ready to retire, or maybe his term is up. He's a political appointee from Washington, D.C., like all district marshals. In his case, he has never been a field man, mainly a lawyer and playing the political game, which has many pitfalls. He's not a friend to Timothy Leighton or the local sheriff. They're often at odds."

"So, he's not a gunfighter or a peace maker?"

"I'm afraid that's the case but he supposedly has several good honorable deputies. They haven't fallen into the lure of money and corruption like the other law enforcement types in the territory."

Marshal Gus O'Reilly showed up about an hour later dressed in an impeccable suit and well groomed. He had a handgun in a shoulder holster under his suit jacket. He had brought along his trusted Chief Deputy, Henry Gutierrez. The chief deputy was well-heeled with a twin .44 caliber revolvers on his gunbelt covered with silver conchos. Luke also noticed the top of a Bowie knife stuck down in his black leather boots.

Luke made introductions and asked everyone to have a seat. He told the participants to relax and if it felt comfortable, use first names. He ordered room service with tea and coffee, and fresh pastries; and set about telling his story about the 3Q Ranch situation. He then led up to the murder of ranch hand Gabe at the Lucky Lady, and then the shooting of Jake by Carlos in defense of Hussong.

Gus nodded a few times. Henry asked a few questions to clarify several parts of the story, and pulled on his bushy handlebar mustache.

Gus said, "I'm sure that you checked on me in Denver or Washington, like I did with you. You came back with a good report. Even Henry was satisfied and he's a tough man to accept a good rating." He chuckled and patted Henry on the knee.

Gus continued, "Here's how we start."

Henry said, "The US District Court has jurisdiction for two reasons: the first is that Arizona is still a US Territory, and also Mexican Nationals are involved like Gregorio, Tomas, and Mrs. Carmen Quinn. That makes it international."

Gus added, "So you'll be seeing us around…maybe ask you some more questions and get any ideas that you might have about Leighton. His name is already familiar in Washington, D.C., and not favorably."

Diecisiete

Again, Leighton was in total reverie as he sat at his desk and studied the rapidly growing city through his bay window. He had just sent a little brunette from Nebraska back to her crib. She had run away from home seeking a more interesting life, and she found her new life quickly when she was snatched from the train station by Leighton's henchmen. The two kidnappers had promised her a meal and a job at a restaurant. Instead she found herself locked up and coached by Mama Vicky into what her new career would be. In the beginning, she was resistant but grew hungry and thirsty, and wanting to see the sun again. The little girl wasn't a virgin so when Vicky introduced her to an older gentleman, she traded her amour for sandwich and a sarsaparilla.

Leighton found her to be a sweet, delightful person and gave a "thumbs up" to her male handler. He also wrote a note to Vicky which said he wanted her reserved and kept fresh for his special government visitors from Washington, D.C.

Benjamin knocked on his door, and Leighton yelled, "Come ahead. The door is open."

Benjamin walked to his desk, followed closely by Billy Jones. Both men tried to talk at one time.

He asked Benjamin to leave, and told Billy to come out with the news. He could see that Billy's eyes were wilder than normal, and he was sweating profusely. His arms kept fidgeting on the tops of his revolvers at his waistline.

Billy said, "Someone killed Jake at the hotel. There were no witnesses, and the desk clerk was out back doing his accounting paperwork. After getting the news, I talked to the stupid sheriff at the scene. He's blundering through an investigation that going no where. I recognized Jake right away – it was definitely him and he took a gunshot right through the head."

"That idiot was getting too big for his breeches anyway. What's your plan? What do you think is going on?"

"It's something to do with the 3Q...I just know it. After I killed Gabe, Jake was supposedly going to find out where he was staying and maybe tie it in with some other 3Q riders. Then he gets killed. Too much coincidence here. I'm going to find out and start killing off some of those drovers."

"Start with the hotel clerk and the desk sign-in sheet. He's not dumb. He'll come around to your way of thinking, like he saw something or someone. I know he's got a beautiful wife – threaten to put her in Vicky's crib. He'll talk."

"Yeah, I know her. I hope he doesn't talk. I'd like to have a go at her, and their gorgeous daughter. She's starting to bud out."

Leighton laughed, "You could have them any time. What's been holding you up?"

Bill answered sheepishly, "Been busy from our last raid coming back from Flagstaff. Brought back several Hopi women and a white lady pilgrim from the Saint Jo wagon train."

"That's a lot of females. How do you find time for robbing and rustling?"

"I know. I had to cut back. I gave the Hopis to Vicky. She says they're very popular among the so-called prosperous elite, like the bankers and even a couple of army generals."

"How about the white gal? Got her tamed yet?"

Billy chuckled, and his eyes got even wider and started twitching, "She's a spit fire, that one. I have to keep her locked up. I calm her down with a spanking, and then promise her food and water. She's submitting now, but it seems too much of a struggle."

"Even for a confirmed rapist like yourself?"

"Yeah, sometimes. But right now, I'm going to talk to the clerk about how Jake got himself shot."

"See you later.   Tell that dumb sheriff I wanna talk to him."

Billy and several of his owl hoot pals strolled over to the hotel to talk to the clerk. The desk was empty, and so was his hotel room where he stayed with his family. Billy asked the Hispanic hall maid where the clerk was. She knew who Billy and his strong-arm pals were. She had seen them beat up hotel guests in the past.

The maid shuddered and started crying. She murmured, "I don't know. They all left about an hour ago. *Madre de Dios*, please don't hurt me."

Billy yelled, "We don't care about you, bitch. We just want the clerk and his wife." He slapped her face, "Tell me where they went or we hurt you!"

One of the owlhoots said, "I can make her tell us."

"No, let her be. She doesn't know. She's totally frightened - she just wet her pants."

The owlhoots checked the train and stagecoach stations with no luck. The rental and boarding stables were also negative. The clerk and his family were gone.

As Billy reported back to Leighton, Benjamin said to hold up a few minutes. They could hear Leighton screaming at the sheriff and telling him to find Jake's killer. He continued, "I want him found and help Billy find that gawd-damn hotel clerk. The clerk saw the whole thing. We need to know if that ranch bunch is here from Tucson."

As the sheriff was backing out of Leighton's room with hat in hand, he kept repeating, "Yes Boss, I understand. I'll get all my deputies out checking the whole neighborhood." His bulbous nose was growing bigger and redder. Likely he had a bottle of booze in his jacket pocket, and he'd be taking a tug before he got to the stairwell.

As he left, the sheriff glanced over at Benjamin and Billy and he quickly looked down. Billy's hard gaze made him walk faster. His shoulders were slumped and his pride was gone. He reminded Billy of the men that he had embarrassed and made back down, causing them to slink away like beaten dogs.

Billy updated Leighton. A few minutes later, Benjamin knocked on the door, and said, "You have visitors, two ladies."

Two huge outlaws pushed Abby and Joanna into the room. The ladies were fresh from the beauty parlor and Abby was wearing a new dress and Joanna had a large red hat with a wide brim covered with rich brocade.

Abby was upset and said to Leighton, "What are you men doing and who the hell are you?"

Relax...we'll find out in due time." He looked at Rudy and asked, "Why are they here?"

"Boss, they've been asking questions about you and your operations in several of the shops. And another thing, they're from Tucson and maybe know that 3Q ranching group."

Leighton calmly asked, "Ladies, are you part of the 3Q ranch. Do you know the owners?"

Joanna couldn't stay quiet any longer. She was not used to being pushed around by any man. She said, "The 3Q is a big ranch outside of Tucson. That's all I know. I run a boarding room – my husband died and I make a living taking in boarders."

Billy asked, his eyes twitching, "What about her?"

Abby answered, "I can speak for myself. I run the stageline from Tucson to Phoenix, some stops along the way and sometimes all the way to Phoenix. It depends on the mail and freight. We're up here for several days doing lady things, like eating too much and pampering ourselves in the beauty parlors. Phoenix seems so much more civilized than Tucson."

"And why the questions about me? Why are you checking me out?"

"You know how girls gossip. We really liked this building and asked who owned it." She paused and added, "We're both single, so we asked if you were married and how old you were. Joanna's a widow-lady and I've never been married." Abby flashed her eyes and smiled. She was flirting like a school girl.

He smiled back. Billy just shook his head. He understood no part of courtship and gentile conversation.

Abby asked, "Well, are you married?"

"No, I'm not married, but I would make a terrible husband. I'm always busy at work and travel a lot."

"Then, are we free to go? I'm staying at the Prospector Hotel if you would like to chat sometime."

"Yep, you can go. But no more questions about me or my operations. My workers get nervous when people start nosing around." And he added, "And Billy gets real jumpy."

Leighton waved Benjamin over to his side. "The ladies are free to go. Please take them to our bakery so they can take a nice cake and cold drinks back to their hotel.'

Abby said, "Thank you, kind sir. We'll be going now." Both ladies curtsied and followed Benjamin out the door.

Billy asked, "I should have them followed, right?"

"Sometimes I wonder about you, Billy. Does a bear shit in the woods? Does the padre wear sandals?"

As Billy made his exit, he was thinking, "What does a bear or padre have to do with the women?" He figured Leighton had insulted him but he wasn't sure. If it turned out to be insult, Leighton would pay the price just like all the rest of his victims. The big ones can fall just as fast, but harder. He always made sure of that!

Dieciocho

After picking up their cake and drinks, the ladies left the building as fast as they could, and once outside each took a deep breath of air. Joanna said, "That was close. The way that Billy kept looking at us, I figured he must be the hatchet man and he was going to use us for axe practice."

"Let's keep walking. You know they'll be following us. We'll pretend to be shopping along the way. We'll go to the Prospector Hotel and check in. I know where it is – about 12 blocks."

"Geez, how many hotels will we be using on this trip? How about a cab?"

"No way, Lady. We need exercise. Have to burn up the sugar from the cake."

As they headed for the hotel, they purposely waltzed in and out of a dozen shops. Abby watched their back trail, and saw the followers duck into store fronts and alley ways.

The Prospector Hotel was a middle grade hotel where Abby had stayed before. They booked one room together. Abby said, "I don't want that Casanova to think he can bound over here to a woman all by herself in her own private room."

Abby had bought a pair of men's pants, a common cowgirl hat, and a wrangler shirt along the way. She told Joanna that she planned to duck out the back, with her hair pulled up under the hat and wearing man's clothing, and make her way to the Mojave Hotel so she could meet with the rest of the land team. She knew Gregorio and Luke would be getting worried because they were already several hours late for the appointed meeting time. She started changing her clothes.

Joanna asked, "What should I do, especially if that Leighton fellow shows up here?"

"If he comes over, which right now is unlikely, just tell him you were napping and I went out to a stage show. You won't know where or what play."

"This is getting more like a dime western mystery every minute. What should I do if there's a problem?"

"Take the candle from the kitchen table and put it right in front of the back window."

"Okay, I think my questions are answered. I do wish I had my 10-gauge shotgun with me, or my dogs. I'd like to have Luke's dog Perro sitting by the front door."

As darkness fell, Abby slipped out through the back. She moved stealthfully and was convinced that she hadn't been seen. She watched the shadows. There was no cigarette glow, or movement, or any noise. She was at the Mojave Hotel in less than fifteen minutes. She had circled the hotel twice and saw no one following her.

Abby slipped into the hotel lobby through a side door and saw that their usually conference room was closed. She tried the handle. It was open. Her fast, covert entry surprised everyone; she was an't immediately recognized and they thought a stranger had moved into their midst. She took off her hat and shook out her blonde hair.

Luke said, "Damn, we've been worried about you and Joanna." Carmen and Alyce hugged Abby dearly.

Gregorio exclaimed, "Where is Joanna? Where have you ladies been – we've been worried sick but hesitant to start looking around. It would have been too obvious."

Luke asked, "Is she safe? We need to go find her and bring her back to our meeting."

Abby related what had happened, and it appeared that they had been found out. She said, "There's a crazy kid that seems to be second in command. His name is Billy, a weird, skinny guy with strange wide eyes."

Luke said to Gregorio, "Now we can see what mercy got us. That little bastard probably got Gabe killed."

Gregorio asked, "What should we do now? I suggest we change our plans and go home. Let the bastards come to us. Right now, we're on their turf and soon they'll know our every move."

Luke agreed, "Time to go home. They'll start picking us off, one by one."

"We're all here right now, except for Joanna. Abby, I want you to take Tomas and Freddy and get the stage and horses ready. Gregorio, you get the ladies organized and ready to roll…and work at getting all our property from the various hotels. We'll get everything ready and start moving back to Tucson just before daybreak. Everybody load and lock."

Abby asked, "How about Joanna? She's in Room 210 of the Prospector Hotel – not far from here. If there's a candle burning in the back window, it means something went wrong."

Grgeorio said, "Don't officially check out of your hotels. We'll pay by bank draft after we get back home. Keep in mind that Leighton has informants every where."

Luke looked at Carlos, and stated, "We'll be taking care of getting Joanna back to this hotel. If we get lucky, maybe we'll run into Billy."

Luke and Carlos pulled their black hats down over their faces and put on their long riding dusters, and each slung a shotgun and rifle hidden inside. They each carried .45 caliber Colt revolvers.

Alyce appeared alarmed. Luke hugged her and said, "Just the nature of the job. You best get used to it. All wives hate this part." He added, "I love you."

She answered, "Me, too. Was that a proposal?"

"We'll talk after we're curled up in front of the 3Q fireplace with a small bottle of certified real blue agave tequila or we can get you a nice bottle of chardonnay."

The members of the team rambled off to their various assignments. Luke said to Carlos, "If the shooting starts in close range, I usually fire off to the left. You take the right."

Carlos guffawed and jokingly said, "Now, if I can remember my right from my left in the heat of a gun fight with bullets flying everywhere."

"And what else?"

"We don't give up our guns, even if there's a hostage. No hesitation trying to figure out what to do next." He added, "I just have a feeling that you're not too emotional in a gunfight. Probably very decisive."

"Been in a few shooting scrapes. Did I ever tell you I was a Mexican captain in Pancho Villa's Army?"

"Bet you were good. Glad you came over to our side."

"What convinced me to leave was the craziness of Pancho raiding in New Mexico and killing all those townspeople. He wasn't drunk, just evil. In fact, I guess I was a deserter. When the shooting started, I just headed to the nearest mountains and hid out until the fools went back to Mexico."

"So you're an army deserter? Is there a reward?"

"Nowadays, they'd probably give me a medal for getting away from Pancho."

Luke said, "There's the hotel now." There wasn't a candle burning in the window but there seemed to be shadows dancing back and forth on the glass as they looked up to the second floor."

"Well, Carlos of Poncho's Army. Here we go." He playfully touched Carlos' right arm, and said, "That's your right, unless we get turned around or start rolling on the floor, then just take out the guy that wants to shoot me."

"It's a deal."

Abby had told them the layout of the hotel. They entered the front lobby and went immediately to the stairway in the back of the front desk. Once on top, they turned to the right, and ran to #210.

They heard screaming and thumping, and probably furniture being broken up. Luke and his partners drew their handguns; and Luke had his shotgun on a sling in easy firing range. They turned the door handle and it opened. In they went, low and precisely searching for targets. Luke took out an outlaw with a double tap to his chest. The man went down. Carlos had found his target and took out his adversary with a single shot between the eyes. Joanna had been stripped naked, and the third outlaw held her in front of him with a .44 caliber revolver pressed against her temple.

He yelled, "Drop your guns or she dies."

Luke casually said as he advanced on the man, "Yeah right!"

The outlaw momentarily looked at Luke at which time, Carlos shot one more rotten outlaw straight through the ear. There was no reflex on the outlaw's trigger finger as he slumped to the floor. Blood splattered all over Joanna. At first she thought she was shot, but managed to say, "I'm still alive."

She ran over to Luke and hugged him. She was bruised and beaten, and had been raped. One eye was closed. Carlos gave her some clothes, and said, "Hurry, get them on. We've got to get out here. That crooked sheriff is probably on the way right now."

She repeated several times, "I tried to put a candle in the window but I couldn't get away."

Luke said, "Don't give it another thought. You did your best. You're alive, right? What else matters right now?"

As they left the room, Luke said, "I've got Joanna. There's probably a lookout in the lobby. Might be a good place to use your shotgun."

"You mean like this?" Carlos held his scattergun in ready position and had six extra shells strapped to the stock."

As anticipated when they reached the bottom of the stairs, a gunsel came out from behind a book case, and stupidly said, "You bastards are going to die." Carlos took him out with both barrels of his shotgun.

The bald clerk ducked down behind the front desk, and yelled, "I'm not part of it." Luke took him by the collar and declared, "If you want to continue living, you didn't see anything. Got it?"

"Yessir. Please let me go." As his body shriveled from fear, his little suit and bowtie looked two sizes too big for him.

They headed out the back of the hotel and criss-crossed their way back to the Mojave Hotel. They weren't followed. Luke placed his duster over Joanna so the desk clerk couldn't see who they were bringing in.

Luke gave him the 'shhhh' sound, winked, and slipped him a silver dollar. The obsequious clerk grinned, "I understand, Sir. Have a good time with your whore."

The ladies were already in the same room and packed up. When they saw Joanna, they quickly cleaned her up and got her some clean clothes. They bandaged her wounds. Abby kept saying that she was so sorry.

Joanna said, "Not your fault. Neither of us expected the horny old Leighton to move this fast." Joanna was crying and recovering emotionally now that she safe. She had moved from hopeless fright into anger and was ready to charge Leighton with shotguns at daybreak.

She asked Abby, "What do you think Doc will do after he finds out what happened. Do you think that he will forget about me after I've been raped?"

"I know Doc. Everything will be fine. He'll help you get your health back and don't worry, things will get back to normal."

Gaining her composure, Joanna related that Leighton had sent the goons to find Abby and to bring her back to the Emporium. Right away, they didn't believe that Abby had gone to the stage show and started beating on her. Two of the miscreants stripped her and raped her. The third outlaw said, "It's okay to bang her. The boss doesn't want this one."

Joanna said that the 3Q Ranch didn't come up in the attacks and there was no talk about Gabe being murdered. Leighton and Billy might have had suspicions but they hadn't quite put the puzzle together.

Luke said, "Time to start moving. Several of you will ride in front of the stagecoach, and Gregorio and I will bring up the rear and watch the back trail. Carlos will ride on the stage as the shotgunner for Abby up front. He's pretty damn good with a shotgun!"

Gregorio asked, "Should we leave a note for Marshal O'Reilly?"

"No need. He and Gutierrez will figure it out. I hope they ride down to Tucson to pay us a visit. We'll need the help."

Luke shouted, *"Vamonos, mis Amigos!"*

Diecinueve

Luke told the crew that they would ride hard from sunrise to sunset. He intended to get back to Tucson in two long days, rather than three, knowing that Leighton and his renegades would be hot on their trail by now. They had seen just a few travelers on the road, mainly prospectors and hard-working cowboys. They even met a writer along the trail who was doing a story on how Tucson compared to Phoenix for a New York newspaper. He had already been to Tucson and found it to be a growing but peaceful community.

Luke said, "There's no time for us to talk right now. You'll probably find Phoenix loaded with vagabonds, thieves, bunco-artists, and other misfits." He added, "I even heard there had been some murders, and the lawmen and politicians were crooked."

"That's news! My name is Roscoe Reeves, journalist. Phoenix sounds like it might be good story material." He was young, enthusiastic and idealistic – probably fresh out of college and on his first big assignment.

"Be careful you don't get caught in the crossfire with the miscreants. There's going to be a lot of fireworks in the next few months. Big land grabs are being staged by a greedy land baron."

"Do you know any names…and places?"

Luke laughed and said, "I don't much about any of that. It might be all gossip. We heard the talk in the saloons."

"Do they have girls and gambling in the saloons? I might want to do a story about that."

"All the western towns have brothels and gambling dens. There's a shortage of women and not much activity for the cowboys and miners on the weekend. So vice activities are very popular. Usually the gambling games are rigged, or they have some slick fellow that can hide cards up his sleeve, or deals from the bottom of the deck. The last joint we were in had five slatternly prostitutes that filled you up with cheap whiskey, and then took everything you had, including your honor. You have to be careful."

The lad had heard none of the words of caution. He was thinking of the ladies when he asked, "Are the whores good looking?"

"Depends on what you want. They're probably very experienced. I don't know for sure. I have my lady friend riding on the stage."

"You mean that big blonde handling the reins? She's dynamite!"

"No, the little Indian gal inside the coach."

"Wow, you're going with an Indian. What's that like? Does she carry a scalping knife?"

"No knife, unless you make her angry. She's nice and smart, and before you ask your next question, she is anatomically correct."

"No offense. I'm happy for you. I hope to see you again." He started to ride off.

"Come see us any time. My name is Luke Quinn, and I own the 3Q ranch. You can find me in the Tucson boarding house, or at the ranch." Roscoe waved back over his shoulder. Luke waved and yelled out, "Watch out for Mickey Finn!"

Gregorio was watching and listening to every word. He was chuckling, "He has no idea who or what Mickey Finn is." Gregorio waved at him also, saying "The poor little greenhorn. We should re-name him EP, short for 'Easy Pickings.' The gamblers and soiled doves will totally enjoy the little fellow and his wallet. He'll be lucky to get out of Phoenix with his underwear intact."

"We were all young once. Hopefully, he'll survive and become wiser, and likely write better stories, kind of like that Mark Twain fellow. I enjoy his California stories."

The group settled down at sunset under a hoary cottonwood tree. There was a fresh water stream running close to the massive tree, bubbling over age-polished rocks, and providing plenty of water for the group and their horses and mules. A colorful hawk was hanging motionless in the sky, with his wings spread wide and the orange of the sunset showing through the fringe of his end-feathers. Luke figured that they might have camped in his favorite hunting spot, or he was just as curious as any other living creature about who else was occupying the earth. Crickets began singing their songs.

Fortunately they had bought a load of vittles. The ladies fixed up a meal for the likes of kings and queens with a giant mulligan stew. In another cast-iron dutch oven, the rich and pungent aroma of boiled cabbage, ham hocks and potatoes permeated the air. Tomas and Freddy had bagged a dozen rabbits and quail and were cooking them over an open barbeque fire. A fresh fruit salad was on the improvised menu for dessert.

Carlos laid out a night watch schedule. There was a nearby hilltop where they could watch and listen for any pursuers. Carlos, Tomas and Freddy took the first shifts. Hussong would spend the night moving about in the hills by him, ready to report any suspicious circumstances.

Luke drew the midnight to three o'clock assignment, and he whispered at Alyce as she was finishing cleaning up the pot and pans. He asked, "How about dropping by the bottom of the hill after my shift is finished. Maybe we could watch the moon and count the stars."

"Well Cowboy. I thought you would never ask. But how about snakes and Gila monsters? They come out at night."

"Not to worry. It's getting cold and they'll be deep down in their holes. Its hibernation time on the desert. However my sweet one, you should bring a blanket. We don't want to bruise your little bottom."

"How about your bottom. I feel like riding a bronco tonight. I'm going to wear my boots and cowgirl hat, and see if I can stay on for 10 seconds."

"Hmmm…that has potential. Have you seen Gregorio and Abby? How are they doing?"

"We girls talked. We did Abby's work. Gregorio doesn't have a shift until three o'clock in the morning, so they left about an hour ago for the ridge above the trail. Those two are a good match."

Luke said, "I'm going to get a few hours sleep, then do a quiet ride around the camp before I take my post. There's still warring Apaches out here. Geronimo busted off the San Carlos Reservation again and he's been on a killing spree. So keep your guns loaded."

"I heard the same thing. By causing all the trouble and violence, the government is getting harsher with all the Indian people. I can understand his resistance. They tried to make him a farmer on parched land. Right now, however, his crazy rampage is hurting all of us. He's even raided and killed his own people when they don't side with him."

"You be very quiet and careful when you come out at three o'clock. Watch for Gregorio – he's my relief."

"You forget I am an Indian. I know how to walk softly. But it would be good if Perro was with us. He hears every sound, even squirrels and chipmunks."

It had been a long day and Luke fell asleep in seconds. He heard Gregorio come back twenty minutes before midnight. He asked if everything was okay.

Gregorio said,"*Muy bien.* All is well. We almost fell asleep under our blankets on the ridge."

"Hear or see anything?"

"*Nada.* Are you going out now?"

"Yeah, I'm just going to do a bareback ride back behind the camp. Freddy and Tomas are on post and they know I'm riding around."

"Have fun amigo. Stay safe. The sandman is calling me. See you at three o'clock."

Luke's shift was uneventful. Sleepiness plays many tricks on a human and he used every mental ploy that he could conjure up just to stay awake. He recounted his past love affairs, and then moved on to his fights with his brutal adversaries that carried knives, guns and clubs. He heard animals in the brush several times, probably a coyote or cougar; but no sign or sounds from an Apache or a Phoenix gunslinger.

Gregorio and Alyce showed up right on time. She had prepared and brought jars of hot steaming coffee and toasted bread with strawberry jam. They talked for several minutes until Alyce said it was time to go. She was carrying two blankets. She smiled and said, "Abby recommended two. One for underneath and one on top when the bodies cool off."

Luke said, "Sounds good to me. Stay sharp, Gregorio."

Luke and Alyce moved behind the hill and fell into each other's arms. She threw her hat off into the brush. Alyce broke loose from the embrace and laid out the bottom blanket. They tore off their clothes, and kissed deep and hard. Their tongues danced. She dropped to the blanket and pulled Luke down to her. Her nostrils quivered from the heady musk of his male scent, and she was soon massaging his growing erection. She murmured, "I can't wait any longer."

She laid back and spread her legs wide and his sword found its sheath immediately. She shivered with pleasure and she sucked him deep which brought a sensation for Luke that felt as though his member was being pulled loose from its roots. She then aggressively pushed Luke over on his back and rode him as promised. She had kept her boots on. Despite her weight on him, Luke arched his back in ecstatic appreciation which set off a whirl of delicious sensations for them both.

After reaching the physical land of Eros and slowly coming back to Earth, bit by bit the joyous lovers felt a glowing aura that neither had experienced for many, many years. They made love one more time and were sated for the moment, and careened deeper to that special feeling called love. It was like a drifting nonexistence and they were the only people left on Earth.

The night zephyrs cooled their bodies, and the curlews high in the trees serenaded their souls. They were safe and in love.

They snuggled and caressed, and Alyce pulled the second blanket over them to maintain their warm cocoon. False dawn was soon upon them and the reality of bright sunlight broke through their ethereal dimension.

They walked to the camp as the preparations were being made for breakfast and saddling up the horses and mules. They were holding hands and carrying blankets still covered with leaves and twigs.

Their friends and family cheered and clapped their hands. Both bowed like actors after a performance. Hussong stepped forward with her hat in his hands, and said, "I think you might have lost this last night in the hills."

It as then that Luke knew that even dark-skinned people can glow red from embarrassment; and he definitely knew his love for this exciting woman was very real.

Packing their saddlebags, Alyce whispered to Luke, "Do you suppose he watched us the whole time?"

"Could be." He chuckled out loud. "Maybe now he will expect too much from his own woman."

She playfully punched him on the shoulder.

On to Tucson and the 3Q Ranch.

Veinte

When Billy brought him the news, Leighton lost his calm cold-hearted demeanor. He yelled and screamed, kicked furniture, and ordered Benjamin to leave and close the door. He turned to Billy and exclaimed, "I rely on you to do the simplest things, and they get all get screwed up. Maybe you're too young and too stupid to do anything right."

On the exterior, Billy stayed calm, but inside his soul, he was ready to blast Leighton to kingdom come. Whenever he took a tongue-lashing from anyone, he was ready to strike out. On that last day in Alabama when his father tried to take a strap to him for having sex with the neighbor's sheep, he vowed that no one would ever beat or disrespect him again. He had killed his father and mother, and little sister, and never looked back. He loved the little girl and was sorry about that. He had been on the run ever since. But no one in Arizona knew about these horrific crimes, not even Leighton and his fellow outlaws.

In an emotional daze, he remembered killing Gabe and how much he enjoyed watching the old man die. He would equally enjoy watching the life ooze out of Leighton, maybe even more.

Leighton asked, "So what happened? I wanted that girl. You knew that. Why isn't she here?"

Billy stuttered while trying to control his anger. He liked the power and money, and the women, while working for Leighton and wasn't about to throw it all away because of one lousy female. He answered, "I sent four of our men to bring her back. Apparently there was a lot of shooting and all four were killed. Three were killed in the girl's room and one in the lobby. It was a damn shame – two of the guys had been on raids with me."

"I don't care about those jerks. We can hire a dozen gunsels more when we want them. They're a dime a dozen – damn riffraff, fully expendable. What does our feeble-minded sheriff say all about this?"

Billy released some mental tension and laughed, "As usual the sheriff doesn't know what the hell he's doing. He couldn't find any witnesses anywhere. He was just happy that two of the dead guys had a bounty, so he's about a thousand bucks ahead."

"I don't care if he collects the bounties. That's part of the job for a sheriff. How about the girls? Where are they?"

"They're gone. Whoever did the killing took the girls."

"How about the desk clerk? Don't tell me he's vamoosed also."

"Afraid so. He took off just like the other clerk at the Mojave Hotel. This guy was single, had no family. He took what he needed from his room at the hotel and just disappeared. Our boys couldn't find him at the stagecoach or train stations."

"Did you check all the stables? The girl said she ran a stagecoach line. Maybe she stored the coach somewhere along with her mules. Get moving, dumbie, maybe you can do something right at last."

Billy touched the butts of his guns. Leighton noticed and said, "Go ahead and do it, dumb shit. There goes all your power and women.

You won't have any more females to screw or beat up, or impress the other renegades how tough you are. Your back-shooting days will be finished. Your bravado is backed by me, don't you get it? You are tied to me and I own you. I will tell you what to do, and when I say, 'jump,' you just say 'how high?' You understand? You make me sick, you sack of shit. Get out of here and find those guys that are irritating me to no end."

"Okay Boss, I'll try harder. I'll get everything taken care of."

Leighton reached over to his bar and poured a large whiskey for himself. He didn't offer one to Billy.

Out of the corner of his eye, Billy knew Benjamin was backing Leighton's play with a shotgun. He awkwardly left the room, making a mental note that when Leighton went down, he would take that gawd-damn Benjamin with him.

Benjamin smiled and commented, "That little weasel was almost up your asshole, kissing away."

"I know. It's just a matter of time until I drop the little prick down a sinkhole to China."

Billy rounded up six of his outlaws, and they went from stable to stable trying to find the girl's stagecoach and mules. At one of their last stops, they hit the jackpot when they found that the woman, Abby, often left her stage with him, and that he had fed and groomed her mules as well as ten other horses that all had individual saddles. He couldn't remember the brands on the horses, but he did recall that two of them had a 30 brand.

Billy asked, "Could that have been a 3Q brand?"

"Yeah, that could have been. I got their horses ready in the dark. They seemed like they were in a big hurry."

"Where were they going?"

"Tucson. They left about 10-12 hours ago."

"How did they pay?"

The stable man said, "They didn't pay. They said Timothy Leighton would take care of the bill. That was good enough for me. He's a big man in these parts."

"Who said that –which one?"

"He was a real handsome guy. He said he was an officer in the Mexican Army and had been on a buying trip to Phoenix. He said he was looking for ranches and land to buy on speculation."

As they started to walk away, the stable man asked, "Is Leighton going to pay me?"

"Probably not, and if you don't shut up, he might burn your stable to the ground."

One of the outlaws said to Billy, "I'm glad it's you telling him about the 3Q scheme and not me. I don't think he'll appreciate what's happened."

But Billy told him, and again, Leighton yelled and kicked over furniture. He broke a full bottle of wine when he threw it at the fireplace, narrowly missing Billy. The outlaw pressed his grubby finger nails into the palm of his hands just to release the tension. He was ready to kill the boss.

But he didn't. In his mind, he decided he needed more time before he killed Leighton and took over his land empire. He pictured himself sitting in a large over-stuffed chair in the center of his saloon, with women at his feet, and the *peons* requesting a moment of his time. He would enjoy watching them begging and crawling.

Leighton asserted, "It's too late to catch up to the coach. They'll be in Tucson in a few hours, so we'll have to bide our time and do it right. We'll kill them all, but I want that Abby woman alive. I still have plans for her."

"What's your move now, Mr. Leighton?"

"Round up a small army of cutthroats and renegades, maybe about fifty. Make sure they're well-armed, and appoint several leaders like sergeants, to keep them under control. Our first stop will be the 3Q Ranch, and we're going to burn every building to the ground, and take all the cattle. That will be the end of ranching for that spread, and then we gradually start the legal process of taking over all the land."

"I understand. I'll get recruiting."

"Also bring me that "Hoyden Jane," that weird tomboy in Vicky's brothel, the one that accommodates the lonely wives. I've got plans for her in Tucson."

Billy said, "You have to careful with that one. You never know what she might do – she's an unpredictable bitch, often stupid and violent."

"Just get her to me." Leighton laughed inside, "The pot calling the kettle black. Billy's crazier that a June bug on a hot lamp."

Veintiuno

The stagecoach and caravan arrived in Tucson at sunset without incident. They had pushed hard all day and were exhausted. They gathered at Joanna's boarding house, and Abby and Alyce went to work preparing baths and helping with dinner. Joanna had left the boarding house in the charge of a lady neighbor who had kept everything first order. She had already started an evening meal for the weary travelers.

Tomas and Freddy took care of the horses and mules. Hussong came riding in shortly thereafter and said that he had spotted a few Apache Indians on their back trail. It seemed that the Indians were hunting for game, and showed very little interest in the stagecoach. He ate a quick meal in the kitchen and was soon off to Alyce's village to tell her people that they should keep Rafael for another two weeks.

Joanna went to her room to rest. Her pain and suffering had worsened as the healing was taking place. A neighbor boy had run and brought Doc back. Alyce heard them talking in her room. She was crying and when Alyce looked through the open door, Doc was holding her in his arms, and calmly patting her on the back. He spoke to her softly and said, "Don't worry, Pretty Lady. I will always support you and be with you." It appeared that Joanna was going to get the support from the man that she loved. Doc gave her a dose of laudanum and she was soon asleep.

Luke, Gregorio and Carlos went to the sheriff, Charles T. Mortimer, to make their report and let him know that he and his deputies should prepare for an upcoming battle. Luke felt that they would be followed by Leighton and his henchmen. He said that Leighton was intent on taking the 3Q, and when he didn't possess Abby that it made his quest personal. They also talked about Billy Jones, the lunatic boy leader. The sheriff pulled out a flyer from his desk. It was now known that Billy was wanted for three murders in Alabama and there was a one-thousand dollar reward, dead or alive.

Mortimer also showed Luke his telegram from US Marshal Gus O'Reilly which said that Deputy Henry Gutierrez and five deputies would be riding over to help out with the Leighton situation. Mortimer asked, "Are they trustworthy. Should we plan and confide in these guys?"

Luke answered, "From everything we've learned, Gus is a political crony trying to survive in the dog-eat-dog political world. But his deputies are straight-shooters and completely reliable – real peace officers."

From everything that was said in town, Mortimer was an honest and courageous man. He had survived the war as a bluecoat major and had worked his way west after a stint as a deputy in Dodge City. In Tucson, he had been elected by a wide margin fair and square. He said that he had five strong, trained deputies, and a dozen reservists who had never been tested in a real gunbattle. They were storekeepers and farmers by trade, and usually only carried guns when they were hunting in the hills.

Luke said, "If they have to defend their town and their families, they will fight as ferocious as any warrior. History is full of stories where local people were written off but organized to beat back organized armies like the Romans in France and Germany. One of the best heroic accounts was where Scotsman William Wallace and his ragtag army defeated an English well-equipped army, and they only had old Claymore swords and clubs; the difference was that they were fighting for their families, land and freedom."

"Maybe the local people won't see it that way. They might decide it's your battle over your ranch, and why should they be killed fighting for a large ranch owner."

"Dictators and bullies never stop at the first boundary. Leighton will want it all, including the town and the farms. They are definely fighting for their own land and families. Remind everyone also that the 3Q Ranch has been sub-divided and is now owned by seven different people and maybe some new wives later on."

"Good to know. Where do you think they'll hit us?"

Gregorio answered, "We don't think we can defend the ranch… too spread out. They'll likely cross the ranch land, burn everything and either steal or kill the remaining cows." He added, "Then I think they'll head for town. They'll be looking for us, maybe at the boarding house, or at Doc's or Abby's stagecoach office…a lot depends on what their informants tell them, and there will be informants. Money talks with immoral, unprincipled people. That's just the way it is."

The sheriff asked, "How about the banks and businesses?"

Luke asserted, "No doubt in my mind that they plan to wreak havoc on the whole town and its people. They'll want to terrorize and scare the holy hell out of everyone. Then the citizens either move or learn to play Leighton's game. Either way, he wins."

Gregorio added, "The way we figure it, they won't be here for three or four days. They've got to recruit a passel of outlaws, get them a pile of guns and ammo, food and water for their livestock, and supplies for the road. Crossing over the 3Q will take a day or two."

Mortimer said, "Today is Wednesday. We can plan a nice town welcome on either Saturday or Sunday." He smiled and said, "If it's Sunday, my wife won't bicker at me about missing church."

The next day, two unlikely strangers moseyed into town. One went to the Happy Days Gentleman's Club, and the other to the Territorial Enterprise newspaper office. Each had a mission.

Veintidos

By Thursday, Billy had organized his outlaw army and made ready to start moving at daybreak. As instructed by Leighton, he had appointed three of the most vicious, brutal renegades as sergeants: Wild Dog Larsen, Claude Russell, and Dirty Dick Smith. He saw them as a pack of boneheads, but he knew that they could keep the others in line and follow his orders. They were promised a bonus and a share of the loot. Secretly, Billy was hoping they'd get killed in the upcoming fights and he wouldn't have to share or worry about his status in the pecking order.

At the last minute, Leighton decided to ride with the outlaws. It was unusual that the boss ever went on the raids. It made Billy nervous. He wondered if someone in the pack had made an alliance with Leighton against Billy. Before leaving Phoenix, he had seen Benjamin jawing with Dirty Dick. He decided he would stay on his guard and watch his back. Sometimes paranoia and total distrust allowed one to live longer.

Dirty Dick had sent scouts ahead to the 3Q Ranch. One renegade Apache, Moon Walker, was particularly good at sneaking through brush, and in a past encounter with the US Army, had actually snuck up on a sentry and tapped him playfully on the shoulder. The soldier thought it was practical joke from a friend, until Moon Walker methodically stabbed him through the throat. The soldier hadn't made a sound, except for a gurgling rush of blood as he died facedown in the hot dust. Moon Walker and his pack of savages then killed six soldiers as they slept nearby.

The Indians reported back that the three line shacks and the main ranch house had been burned to the ground. There was a cabin remaining above the main ranch house. It was occupied by several families, about twenty with wives and children, of the Apache Chiricahua Clan, possibly part of Geronimo's families. They had gathered some cows and horses in corrals and it looked like they were planning on staying through the winter. Moon Walker was a heartless killer from the White Mountain Apache Clan and had no respect for the other clans, actually for any human being. Billy and he made equitable sociopath working partners.

Moon Walker gave the information to Leighton who simply said, "Kill 'em all. Then burn the cabin to the ground. Kill the stock."

Even Billy was momentarily shocked. "Even the little children?" He was thinking back on his murdered little sister.

"Billy, kill them now, or in fifteen years. What's the difference? Those children will come for you in a few years, and it won't be to sit down and have a powwow."

Hussong lay on his belly on the ridge above the cabin. He watched the outlaws and the Indian scouts move towards the cabin. There was no stopping the attack without being killed himself. He could do little good in warning the families. It was one of those slow-moving events in nature that seems to be part of the scheme of things, like an earthquake, flood, or prairie fire. The surprise attack was brutal and savage, most of the people being killed with knives and hatchets. Two of the warriors managed to fire their rifles three or four times, and one outlaw was stopped in mid-air by a shot to the chest and he went to meet his maker. One young woman fought like a grizzly bear when her child was clubbed but she was subdued from behind by another outlaw with a club.

From his vantage point, Hussong saw a small boy hiding above the cabin. He had a child's bow and arrow, and had probably been practicing his hunting skills. He watched the raiders annihilate his family but he stayed still and didn't break cover. He could be saved if he didn't move.

The Indians kept a few of the horses, and the outlaws went about shooting the cows and the remaining horses through the head. The renegades then dragged the human bodies into the cabin, and set it ablaze. Within minutes, the cabin was a raging inferno fed by its own heat and oxygen, and by the human bodies.

From beginning to end, it had only taken about thirty minutes to kill twenty-two people and destroy the livestock. There was an older man with a white beard riding a thoroughbred Arabian stallion. Hussong spotted Billy Jones in the milling outlaws and Indians. He seemed to be in charge and was giving orders. Hussong was wishing that there hadn't been so many raiders – he had several clear rifle shots to take out the bastard. He had to purposely remove his itchy finger from the trigger. The renegades mounted up and moved on towards Tucson, leaving death and destruction in their wake.

Hussong knew that he had to alert Luke and the others quickly, but first he had to rescue the boy. The lad appeared frozen in place, and Hussong was quietly able to come up behind him. He put his hand over the boy's mouth, and whispered "friend" in several different dialects. He felt the boy relax, so he understood. He didn't scream or try to run away. He was probably too traumatized except to go along with Hussong and hope for the best. Hussong called up his horse and together they would ride to Tucson. They could easily beat the outlaws to town – he knew the shortcuts and wasn't loaded down with gear and fire power.

There was another survivor who patiently observed Hussong and the boy from behind a boulder abutment. Her name was Flower Petal and she was the lad's auntie. She had been gathering pine nuts for the winter. She assumed that the boy would be safe with the Hopi and she slipped off into the woods to find Geronimo. She had water in a leather bag and a pouch filled with nuts and jerky. After climbing down from the mountains, she stopped to rest by a spring-fed lake. Revenge hung in the air like morning fog over the chilly lake.

It would be a long walk across the desert but she was determined to seek vengeance on the outlaws and the traitor Indians. Her husband and a granddaughter were among the dead. The brave warrior leader, Geronimo, would know the way to seek justice.

She walked at early sunrise under a bright canopy of stars. Flower Petal knew she lived in the world of nature, savage at times and survival was often tough, but in all her years and sitting with the wise elders, she could never understand human cruelty to one another.

But then again, it was possible the Great Spirit didn't care about a few human lives. Humans were mere grains of sand on the earth, and the sun was only a small star in the million of others in the limitless universe.

Veintitres

In Tucson, Hoyden Jane took a temporary job at Lucille's Happy Times before the day was out. Most of the brothels catered to men but Lucille had specialized services for certain wives who wanted anonymity and a chance to explore their sexuality. Jane was slender and lithe, and most of the mature ladies found themselves holding and treating her like a child. Sometimes they spanked her for being naughty. The games often took imaginative directions. The foolish ladies should have known that they would expect blackmail before they enjoyed their first climax. As with men, the sex drive made risk takers out of normal, church-going ladies.

Jane knew how to exploit the women with their hoity-toity reputations and their social status in the community. Jane wanted information about the banks for Timothy Leighton. She had done this kind of work before and he had always given her a nice bonus. Lucille had contacted two ladies about Jane and had told them that "a new young girl" was at the brothel. Her first customer was Georgiana and her husband was the owner and manager of the Arizona First Trust Bank. She also had an appointment later in the day for another woman, Georgiana's friend, who had heard about the new lady and she entered at the back entrance of the brothel. Georgiana had paid Lucille up front for both ladies.

When Jane talked to her lesbian friends in Phoenix, she said that she could write an instruction manual for future lesbian workers. She said it would be very similar to men in many ways; their love partner didn't understand them; the partner was too busy to show them much attention; the partner was rough and gruff and didn't make the effort for total satisfaction; the partner was dull and didn't want to explore all the rituals of Venus; and of course, the best part, the client herself was not a lesbian and had never done this sort of thing before.

Jane was impressed with Georgiana. She was beautiful and well-dressed, just a wee bit overweight, and giggled when she said that she had forgotten her pantaloons. As expected, she complained about her husband and made it clear that she was not a lesbian. She was eager to make love and wanted to explore her sexuality. They were naked in bed within twenty minutes. Jane knew lovemaking was her job but she often enjoyed her work. Georgiana was a wonderful kisser.

After both ladies had climaxed, it came to the point that Jane least liked, but it had to be done. Georgiana was massaging her slim, athletic body when Jane said, "I have to tell you something. I hate to do this. You're a wonderful lover, but I need to know all about your husband's bank. My friends are going to rob it in a few days. No one will get hurt if you give me all the details and no one needs to know what happened today. Lucille is very discreet – that's how she stays in business in a small town."

Georgiana stiffened, and started to cry. She thought to herself that if Lucille hadn't kept her mouth closed, she would have been found out a long time ago. She mumbled, "I knew this was going to happen one day." It was now clear to Jane that this was not Georgiana's first time with a lady friend. After some persuasion, she admitted the lady coming in later for an appointment was a close friend from her college dormitory days, and they had been intimate. They apparently were not jealous of each having other lovers or their husbands taking them to bed. She sobbed, "Marie is her name. What should we tell her about all this?"

"You don't have to tell her anything. I'll take care of it. I'll let her enjoy herself and then I'll tell her like I told you. I know her wealthy husband owns another bank – I just need the information. No one needs to know about me or you two ladies together.

Understood?"

"No one will get hurt? I still love my husband in my own way and we have two children together."

Georgiana drew a map of the layout of the bank, where the money was kept, and explained how the vault was open during the day. No one had ever anticipated a possible holdup and caution was thrown away like yesterday's garbage.

"I guarantee no one will get hurt. They just want the cash." She crossed her fingers behind her back. She knew how cruel Leighton and his gunsels could be. She had seen them destroy a girl's face at one of the Phoenix whorehouses for stealing from a VIP customer.

The afternoon with Marie was as equally delightful as the morning with Georgiana. She wasn't as alarmed as Georgiana about being found out. She said, "I'll tell you what you need to know, but I'm tired of hiding and being secretive. When this is all over, I might leave my husband and move away and start a new life."

"How about Georgiana? Wouldn't that break her heart?"

"She could come with me. Her children are grown. We could start over or go back to the way it was in college. We had four fun, exciting years together at college. I was one of the few students that didn't want to graduate."

As instructed, Marie drew a map and a time schedule of the US Mutual Bank's activities. She also drew a map with the location of Joanna's boarding house, the sheriff's jail, and Abby's stagecoach office.

She tried to pay Jane but Jane said Georgiana had already taken care of the bill in cash. She wanted to leave a tip but Jane wouldn't accept the money, saying "I enjoyed myself as much as you fine ladies." She added, "Please don't try anything stupid like going to the sheriff, or some body may get hurt."

Lucille had arranged for Jane's horse to be out front with her saddlebags full and Jane left one hundred dollars for the use of the bed. Lucille also kept the service fee for the ladies. Lucille had done business with Leighton before and he was usually straightforward and not overly stingy when it came to money. Jane left for her appointment with Leighton and the crazy Billy at sunset. She had the maps and schedules for the upcoming robberies. She had no intention of staying with Leighton's ruffians and planned on returning to Phoenix. She figured that living out under the desert sky with cougars and marauding Indians was better than spending an hour with the motley bunch of outlaws.

About the same time, a young man left the Territorial Enterprise looking for Joanna's boarding house. He was the novice writer from New York and was searching out Luke Quinn. Luke and Alyce had just finished a delightful afternoon with full body massages, and it was time to start preparing dinner. Joanna was back doing light kitchen work. Alyce answered the knock on the front door. She recognized Roscoe Reeves right away. She chuckled to herself that the avaricious painted ladies in the Phoenix saloons hadn't stolen his suit or even his silver pocket watch and writer's canvas bag.

With his face lit-up with enthusiasm, he said in a very slow tempo, "My name is Roscoe. I need to talk to Mr. Luke Quinn." He paused and continued, again very slowly, "Can you help me? I need to find Luke." He talked louder and more precise, thinking if the volume was up, that the comprehension would be more complete.

Alyce shrugged her shoulders, pretending that she knew no English. She gave him her best blank stare. Abby came around the corner and said, "You must know the Navajo language if you wish to talk to her and stop yelling at her."

"I'm sorry. I'm not yelling at her. I know no Navajo. Maybe I could draw some pictures on my pad." He reached inside his canvas bag and took out a pad and pencil.

Abby said a few words in gibberish, looked away and pretended to be disgusted. Alyce answered back in gibberish and raised her voice. She twisted her head from side to side.

Abby said, "Here you are in Navajo land, and you can't speak the language. Alyce wants to know why she has to learn English when you can't even talk to her in the local language."

Roscoe exclaimed, "I know. Again, I'm sorry. Please tell Alyce I will try and learn in my spare time."

Alyce and Abby both spoke some more gibberish, and then Alyce said, "Okay this time, Roscoe. You're forgiven."

Surprised, Roscoe said, "You speak English?"

Alyce replied, "Well, I should hope so after eight years of schooling on the reservation and also working with federal officials."

"Good, we can talk. You can give some insight on what is happening in Arizona from the Indian perspective."

"It's a deal but you have to decide if you want the perspective from the Apaches, Yaquis, Hopis, Navajos, Pueblos, Comanches, etc. viewpoints I can only relate what I know and feel from my personal outlook. There are many tribes here just as in Europe, there are many countries and languages."

"Point taken. May I speak to Luke? Trouble is coming his way from Phoenix."

"We know. We're ready."

Roscoe asserted, "It's pretty serious. Leighton has rounded up over fifty outlaws. They look like a scruffy, motley crew of killers and miscreants. They are mean and dangerous with hundreds of guns. I saw some of them in Phoenix."

Abby called up the stairway for Gregorio and Luke. She arranged a sitting area and table near the end of the dining room, and prepared coffee and tea. She laughingly said, "No tequila today, boys. We have to stay steady."

Roscoe relayed what he had seen and heard in the saloons and in chitchat at the general stores. There was nothing new, except the fact that Leighton had decided to ride with the gang. Roscoe had already told the local newspaper and had telegraphed his home office about the upcoming raids. It was a big chance to become famous. It would be a chance to write about real gunfights, just not read about them in dime novels.

Excitably, Roscoe said that it appeared that Leighton was making his big move to take over the entire state. He said it was shaping up like the beginning of another Civil War.

Luke said, "Roscoe, that's a bit of exaggeration. There'll be a lot of shooting and killing, but there won't be another Civil War. The people are tired of the bloodshed and now in general favor one united country. Slavery is no longer an issue. Leighton will be stopped and very soon. He's out of touch with the feelings of the citizenry. He's just riding along on a power-trip fantasy."

"You know about a crazy kid named Billy Jones? He's a leader of the gang."

Luke smiled, "Yeah, we know Billy. But if Leighton is like most dictators and gang leaders, Billy will likely not survive the battles. He'll catch a bullet in the back. The bosses use a wild card like Billy for what they need, and then quash him like a bug before he gets too hungry for the top job."

Perro barked at the back door. Hussong came in carrying a small Indian boy. The boy looked frightened as his big brown eyes scanned the room. Hussong said, "Luke and Alyce, I found a present for you out on the trail." The boy saw Alyce, a dark-skinned woman in the midst of white faces and ran to her, like she was his mother or auntie.

Alyce picked him up and hugged him and asked, "Where did you find this handsome boy? Why is he so frightened?"

Hussong smiled, "And hungry too. We rode straight in from the 3Q." Hussong told the story about the slaughter of entire families at the cabin, how he saw at least twenty people murdered and how he managed to save the boy while the boy was hidden and quiet on the side of the mountain. "He probably saw his own mother and father butchered. Now he has no home or family, and can't survive on his own, so I brought him here. Maybe you could adopt him."

"I would love to. I have a daughter but a boy in the family would be nice." She looked over at Luke, straight on with a full focus on his eyes. She was looking for approval.

She sighed when he said, "Sounds good to me. He a fine-looking boy, but first we'll have to see if any of his living kin want him back. He's an Apache, and we're a bunch of Navajos and Hopis, and Mexicans and Irish in this house."

Abby interjected, "Don't forget the Swedes and Germans. Maybe that's what he needs –an all-American family."

Alyce inquired, "What should we call this handsome boy? We need to have a good name for him. Hussong said the boy wants a new family name."

Carlos had walked in and said, "I suggest *Jesus*. He is a blessed one right from the Almighty. He has *tengas suerte* – good luck. He is a survivor. He will go on to great things in life."

Both Luke and Alyce nodded in approval. Luke said, "That's a good name for our new family member." Often her face expressed no or little emotion, but when she heard Luke she jumped for joy with Jesus cradled in her arms.

The boy had no idea what was happening or why they were staring at him, except when Alyce sat him at the table, put out some toast and soup, he knew he had found a new home. He ate voraciously, like any young lad who hadn't eaten for over twelve hours. They started calling him Jesus – the boy had heard about the Christian church from his family members that had been on the reservation. He liked his new name. It was a powerful name for anyone. He didn't know about the details of the cross and the Bible, but figured he would learn soon enough, right after another piece of toast.

Veinticuatro

Flower Petal had walked long and hard trying to find Geronimo and his band. She knew that she would not make it on foot to the Indian stronghold way south, but she hoped that another Apache might find her and give her food and water, and directions, or carry a quick message to Geronimo.

She walked and walked, following the general direction of south, by watching the sun in the day and the stars at night. Her grit and gumption kept her going, and her strong desire to avenge the loss of her family. Her water and food were soon gone, and she found no source of water. She ate a few seeds from various plants and sliced open a cactus for liquid.

The last thing she remembered before collapsing was how it was with her family when she was young and carefree, and not worrying about other hostile tribes coming on their land, or the US Cavalry riding in and forcing them to live where they didn't want to. She had heard that sometimes the Indian Agency made the Apaches move to Oklahoma or Florida. Some had died because of diseases to which they had no resistance.

She saw her mother and father in a vision high in the sky, and saw her sisters and friends floating on air behind them. Her father was riding his favorite brown and white war pony. They were laughing and singing the old songs. Her practical brain said they were all dead, but she knew the brain was wrong. She could sense them, and her father talked to her in her teenage years about becoming an adult. Her mother had taught her weaving and basket-making, and she often went fishing in the Gila River with her brother and friends. For some reason, she saw Geronimo on the shore waving. He said, "Don't worry, Flower Petal. It will be okay. I promise."

Then her mind began blackening and fading out. Her thoughts were about dying, and floating through the sky with her ancestors. In a last moment of desperation, she fought to stay alive and declared to the Almighty, "I can't die yet. I must find the killers of my family." But her long plight had taken its toll, and she fell into the dark abyss of darkness, still struggling to live on.

A white gentleman farmer came by in an old rickety wagon. He spotted a small supine figure under a saguaro tree. He wasn't sure it was a human being so he stopped to find out. It was Flower Petal, barely breathing. She was hot and dehydrated. He gave her a drink from his canteen and put a wet cloth on her forehead. She came to and tried to grab the water from him. The farmer said, "Easy does it. You must let your body recover at a slow pace." Her eyes began to focus and she was able to sit up. Her muscles weren't hydrated yet and ready to move.

He picked her up and put her on his wagon, and carried her in back for about thirty miles over the rough bumpy road. He gave her food and water every half hour. She made a quick recovery and pointed south. She knew no English but using sign language, she told him about the *ladrones* and that she was searching for Geronimo. The man had to turn east to his farm, hoping that he wouldn't run into the Apache leader. She knew she had to continue further south to the Indian stronghold.

Joe Race

As she stepped down from the wagon to continue her journey, they were suddenly surrounded by six Apache warriors, all carrying Winchester rifles. They were painted for war and belligerently pointed the rifles at him. One of the warriors had a three-pointed buck tied on the rump of his horse.

Flower Petal cried out in Apache, "No, don't hurt him! He is my friend. He is helping me find Geronimo." She and the leader, Gera, of the warriors talked back and forth, and finally the warrior said in English, "Thank you, White Man, for helping my sister."

Incredulously, the man asked, "She is your sister? Did she tell you about the slaughter on the 3Q Ranch?"

The warrior answered, "We are Apache, all brothers and sisters. Yes, she told me about the killings. I will take her to Geronimo, and he will decide how we seek revenge. He is hiding over twenty miles away."

The farmer man said, "The outlaws that did this are violent, vicious men. They are killers, lawbreakers, and are not like the many decent ranchers and farmers in Arizona. Please ask Geronimo to seek out only the criminals, and not satisfy the blood vengeance by killing innocent wives and children."

"I will tell him. Flower Petal will explain what has happened, but revenge will be ours. This crime will not go unpunished."

Gera waved the white man away. "You are free to go. You and your family will not be harmed."

The leader told two of his warriors to search out the outlaw gang and report back. "They are probably heading for Tucson and may be camped on the outskirts of town. Do not make contact – be invisible. We want to surprise them in our special way."

The two warriors rode off. He said to Flower Petal, "You are a strong woman. We will join Geronimo at his campfire. He has a new young wife from the reservation. I think you will like her."

They reached Geronimo's camp in about fifteen minutes. The leader had said twenty miles so that no one could find Geronimo and even in idle gossip, his camp wouldn't be compromised.

The leader introduced Flower Petal to Geronimo but he could see that the two knew each other. Geronimo said, "We are cousins and spent many days on the San Carlos Reservation and swimming in the Gila River. I knew many of the people that were murdered by the outlaws. We will ride at dawn."

Flower Petal thought, "He is older but still very strong. I see strength and power in his face and know now why the people follow him. He speaks with commitment. It is good that he has a new wife. His first wife and children had been killed in a raid by the US Army."

She stated, "I would like to go and avenge my family. I want to ride with the warriors. You have seen me fight for our home."

Geronimo said, "It is not possible. Women protect the home. Women do not ride into battle."

"They killed my family…our family. I want to face the killers in the battle of vengeance. I deserve to be there."

"I understand. You make a good argument. It is settled. You can ride but first get food and nourishment, and sleep so that you are refreshed for battle. It will be a tough fight. There will be no quarter. Our warriors may die. The outlaws have many weapons and many bullets, and they live by the gun."

Gera said, "It is so but we have the strong and powerful Apache spirits and gods riding with us. Geronimo, I will absorb your magic. You have been invisible before and never been shot in battle. It will be so again."

It was the blackest of nights. The moon had set early and the stars were increasingly masked by thick clouds, outlined in strange shapes and sizes. The horses and cows were making mournful sounds, like eerie spirits were floating through the corrals. The center fire was built higher, and the men began to dance. Frightening shadows formed against the rock wall and the large mesquite trees. The dancers made guttural noises, and kicked up dust with their thumping moccasins.

The warriors painted their faces for battle, and told of legends of the past when the Apache Nation was invincible and would last through eternity. They checked and re-checked their weapons and sharpened their knives. Many went and made love with their wives – some for the last time. Gera had wild, unrestrained sex with both his wives and felt even more virile and ready for combat.

The two scouts reported back, pulling a lone, saddled horse behind them on a lariat. There was a rifle in the scabbard, and a small .32 caliber pistol with some female clothing in the saddlebag. They said that the outlaws were camped a few miles out of town. They were drinking heavily and some were brawling. The scouts said a lone rider had ridden into the camp from town, showed an envelope of messages to an old bearded man who appeared to be the main boss. He ate a meal and then rode out slowly towards Phoenix. The rider camped about an hour later. For whatever reason, it seemed that he didn't want to stay with the gunsels.

The scouts said that since the rider was with the outlaws they decided to kill him while he slept – one less gunslinger to worry about. Using skills they had learned as children, it was too easy. They made the advance on the small, improvised camp, and cut the throat of the rider while he slept. There was little sound, just blood and gore oozing into the sand. They soon learned after stripping the body that the rider was a female. They brought all her clothes, soaps and perfumes back for the camp women. They left her body for the vultures.

By daybreak, Geronimo and twenty armed warriors were riding towards the outlaw camp. Geronimo hadn't decided if he would charge them before Tucson, or wait until they left town and their numbers were less and weakened after fighting with the other white men.

Flower Petal had cut her long black hair and flattened her bosom with wraps of cloth cut from the dead woman's blankets. She carried the woman's rifle and pistol. Her first shots would be directed at the old boss man and then the ugly looking kid who seemed to be a leader of the hired guns.

She felt empowered. The spirit of victory had entered her soul. She felt no fear.

As they reached the top of the ridge over the outlaw camp, Geronimo saw that the main body of outlaws had already left for Tucson. There were three supply wagons still in place with only three guards. Geronimo decided it was sensible to charge the camp and destroy what the main body had left in reserve. The guards were busily cleaning up after breakfast and loading up bedrolls and other supplies. Geronimo still marveled at how foolish white men could be, letting down their vigilance. Not one of them was watching the hills, and Geronimo figured that they had been silhouetted several times when one of the warriors went to the top of the ridge to look closer.

Geronimo sent six of his strongest warriors on the fastest of horses to the camp. Two of the guards were cut down in minutes before they could run but an older man was taken prisoner as he frantically searched for his rifle. One of the warriors interrogated him about the outlaws' plans. Little new was learned.

Geronimo gestured for Flower Petal to come forward. Words were spoken in Apache. She nodded her head. The old man foolishly thought that the talking was about to save him. But he was wrong – dead wrong.

Flower Petal reached inside her vest and pulled out the dead woman's .32 caliber pistol. As he pled for his life, Flower Petal rapidly shot the old man twice, one shot in each eye. He slumped to the ground dead.

Geronimo had his warriors pull the wagons close together and set them ablaze. He allowed the horses to run free. Gera asked, "Do you want to burn the bodies?"

"Strip them and get their guns and ammunition. Leave the bodies in the hot sun to blister and rot. It will be a message for others."

He asked Flower Petal, "Do you want to go back to our camp now?"

"I am only beginning."

In his wisdom, Geronimo knew, "Never underestimate a woman, especially an angry woman."

Gera yelled to the warriors, "Let us settle the score for our people." As they slowly rode towards Tucson, hundreds of bullets were flying in every direction, the cartridges being set off by the fires in the supply wagons. If they managed to escape Tucson, the outlaws wouldn't find food or ammo on their return trip to Phoenix.

Veinticinco

Deputy Marshal Gutierrez and his colleagues rode all night and came into town on the east side. They were dog-tired but tough seasoned men. They had been tested by the elements and the criminals that seemed to flock west when it was "too hot" in the Eastern cities. Routinely, the urban criminals were without sentiment or common sense, and would ruthlessly kill over an ounce of gold or just for pure meanness.

The federal deputies had seen the fires of the large outlaw camp about five miles west of the town limits. As they eased into town, they found the boarding house as previously described by Luke and made contact with Luke and Gregorio several hours before daybreak. Joanna and Alyce made a huge breakfast with gallons of coffee for the marshals. The windows had already been covered with blankets and barricades set up in front of the doors. Luke noticed that Jesus was following Alyce everywhere she went. He helped carry the plates of breakfast to the men. In turn, Perro would follow Jesus waiting for a dropped morsel of food.

Luke said, "Gregorio and I have been planning and strategizing. We think the owlhoots are coming in soon, and killing and terrorizing as many as they can, especially looking for anyone associated with the 3Q. However, Abby picked up information from the town gossips that a lot of questions were asked about the banks. Somehow or another, one of the banker's wives got blackmailed and she's decided to come clean and tell the truth. She's afraid that her husband and friends may be killed."

Gutierrez asked, "What do you want us to do, Senior Deputy Quinn?" He handed deputy badges to Luke, Gregorio and Carlos. "Marshal O'Reilly wanted you men to have these and make sure I swore you in as official deputies."

Gutierrez laughed and raised his hands like he was blessing them as church members, and said, "You men are now duly sworn official-like. That makes me feel as *importante* as a priest at mass."

Luke said, "I still have my retirement badge, so I guess I am now double-official."

"That's why I called you Senior Deputy Quinn."

Gregorio declared, "Now back to business. Gutierrez, if okay with you, we would like you federals to protect the banks. You have a total of six deputies, counting yourself, three to each bank. I'm going to assign Freddy with you and Tomas with the other team. They're both young and need guidance and someone to slap them straight if they get too brave."

"Are they good with firearms?"

"Oh yeah, no problem there. I taught Freddy well. Carlos has taught Tomas with the basic traditions of preserving democracy. To maintain peace and civilization, you must stand firm and be armed. An armed man will stop an unprepared, unarmed man about one hundred percent of the time or turn him into a slave. Freddy and Carlos know that." He added, "Like any town, there will be lily-livered pacificists out on the street today, people who will not fight, even for their families and land. I guess some cowards are meant to be slaves."

He paused, "But Freddy has a bad habit of stopping bullets. He's been hit twice in less than a month, but he's a lucky lad. He has an angel following him around."

Gutierrez chuckled, "I'll watch him close. Maybe the angel will protect me. Then again the poor angel might get embarrassed if she follows me too closely. I hope the angel likes cold beer"

"Or maybe the angel was bad and now has reformed, and gone to heaven. You might learn a thing or two."

Gutierrez smiled. "What's the rest of the plan?"

Luke answered, "We have four ladies in the boarding house and three dogs. The dogs will hear every sound and alert the ladies. All the women have rifles and shotguns and are excellent shots. Gregorio's mother, Carmen, is particularly good with a shotgun. Several of the outlaws have already learned this."

Gregorio continued, "Our town Doc will be here at the boarding house and he can respond wherever he might be needed." He asked, "What is Doc's name anyway? Does anyone know?"

Doc walked in about this time for his breakfast. Of course, he had kept Joanna company upstairs just in case she needed some "special treatment." He said, "Doc's good enough. Some body might tell the bill collector back in my Connecticut home town and they'll come out to Arizona and make me pay up."

Carlos said, "I know. I saw his mail one day at the post office. You best tell, Doc. I couldn't pronounce the last name." Carlos must been excited about the upcoming battles – he was talking without a reason. His adrenaline was already pumping.

"Okay then. In case something happens today that could seal me tight in a pine box, here goes – drum roll and trumpets blaring please. It's Horace Winkelholz. It's even on my college diploma. All through college, I was known as "Winkie" or "Winkie-Dinky." Not good nicknames for a man out west."

Alyce was listening and looked puzzled. Luke patted her on the knee, and said, "I'll explain later. You won't find the term in any language dictionaries."

Gregorio added, "Here's the rest of the plan. The newspaper man tells us that there's about fifty of these yahoos, all mean and armed coming for a visit to our little town. You federals saw their fires. We have a reception planned from the roof tops. Gregorio will be on the north side of the main street, and I'll be on the south. We'll each have four men with us – all armed with Winchesters and good shots. Carlos and Hussong will be staying loose, going from place to place waiting for a spot where they might be needed.

Gutierrez asked, "Where's the local sheriff in all of this? What's he doing and how many deputies does he have?"

"Let's ask him."

Sheriff Charley Mortimer rode up in front with four deputies that Luke had never seen before. He walked into the boarding house and introductions were made. He said that recruiting men for a dangerous mission against well-armed and desperate outlaws had not been easy. He argued with his reservists that arming the people, the tyrant will fall. He declared that free men, well armed and determined would create a considerable risk to the outlaws. Criminals usually prey on the weak and when they meet resistance they usually back down and run away.

Mortimer said that only four of his reserve deputies would commit. The others were either too busy or their wives were adamant that couldn't help out. He understood – the men had families to support and farms and ranches to maintain. Counting himself, Mortimer now had 10 deputies to help out. Luke had earlier discussed him maintaining the jail and sheriff's office and to be prepared for a sudden influx of new prisoners. Mortimer also volunteered to put three deputies at Doc's Office to protect his clinic and to take care of the injured.

Gutierrez added that they shouldn't take any of the outlaws wounded to Doc's office. "The criminals would only escape and continue to cause havoc, and maybe do some more killing and looting. It would take deputies away from the defense of the town." It was agreed that injured outlaws would only go to the jailhouse *carcel*. Gutierrez continued, "You have be extremely careful with these cockroaches. They are not ordinary people and will do anything to survive. Sheriff, I suggest that you relay all this information to your reservists and maybe your newer deputies, do not take any chances. If you have to, shoot the bastards two or three times, and watch for hidden guns and knives."

Luke added, "This comes from experience. Because the jasper says he gives up, don't believe him until he is neutralized completely, like shot between the eyes or handcuffed and hogtied. They'll kill you while you're tending to their wounds and trying to help them. They think and act like rats – anything to survive!"

Veintiseis

Timothy Leighton called to his mob of miscreants to stop about a mile from town. He said," It's time to get organized before we tear this town apart." He started to review the assignments in town.

"Billy, I want you at my side." Leighton was increasingly concerned about a "random" shot in the back of his head. Billy had been talking back to him, arguing, and challenging.

"Wild Dog, you take the First Trust Bank, and Claude, you've got the US Mutual Bank. The doors should be opening just as we hit town. Go in fast and clean them out. Shoot any bastards that get in your way. We have to teach the "good citizens of Tucson" that we are the new officials. And everyone remember, we re-group at the boarding house. We'll make that our headquarters. Dirty Dick will be going back and forth in the operation, but mainly to keep our guys moving from place to place, and handling resistance when it develops."

Dirty Dick nodded and then yelled out, "Hey, what's that smoke back at our camp?"

Leighton answered, "Damn! Whatever it is, it's not good. Might be Indians or the 3Q owners came in behind us. They probably got our extra ammunition. We've got no choice now. We gotta subdue this town and make it our headquarters for our future plans."

Billy said, "I'm going to send a rider back to see what's going on and then report to us in town."

"Good, send Bo. He's fast, clear-thinking, and has a good horse."

Billy told Bo to get moving and get to him with a report at the first bank in town. Bo took off like streaked lightning in the direction of the smoke. As soon as he was out of sight of the outlaws, he made a direct line to the north. He figured he wasn't about to become bait for the Apaches and decided he would go to Flagstaff and maybe find a job riding the range. He had been embarrassed and slammed around by Billy, and knew it would just be a matter of time before they had a fatal shootout. And he knew it wouldn't be a fair fight – Billy was a back shooter and bushwhacker. He laughed to himself, "I've got too much living to do. I want to have some more pretty women." Since it was a cowboy town, Bo figured there would be lot of available ladies, hopefully Latin ladies with the big breasts. He had learned the words he needed for the Mexican prostitutes – *putas*, brothel – *burdel*, and course, plenty of *dinero*.

Bo had just saved his own life twice all in one day. He missed the Apaches and the deadly firefights in Tucson…and he would have a chance to find some more pretty women. Actually when he re-considered, make it thrice saves – Billy wouldn't be shooting him in the back.

Even if the town hadn't been alerted about the outlaws' raid, the dust cloud of over fifty riders, led by Leighton, Billy Jones and Dirty Dick, coming in from the west would have awakened the deafest and dumbest of the townsmen. Even after all his working years, Luke was continually astounded by the stupidity and arrogance of the outlaws. He had expected them to drift into town a few at a time, and then organize for their raping and pillaging. However, Leighton was accustomed to everyone being weak and subservient to his every command. Although Leighton was brazen and threatening, from his perch high atop the general store building, Luke figured the odds would be in the defenders' favor. Thinking ahead, the roof top defenders had placed long wooden planks from building to building so they could move back and forth as the battle lines changed.

Luke yelled over the side, "Okay, everyone take your posts and pick your targets carefully and make every bullet count."

Luke watched the townspeople scurrying from post to post, jacking in rounds in their rifles and making ready for the battle. He knew the outlaws made their living with their guns; they were experienced and had no compunction about shooting another human being. He wondered how many would die on either side. He was sure that experienced lawmen like the sheriff, Gutierrez and himself had come to grips that any day, maybe today, would be the day that they paid the piper for all their dangerous work.

Luke carried five scars on his body from previous close calls. He knew he had outlived his odds, but now he had a reason to live on, desperately wanting to stay alive. He wanted to settle down with Alyce and her daughter and the new addition, Jesus.

Luke put all these emotions on hold; they would only distract him. He was now into the lawman's survival zone. He thought, "I do not die. They die. It is my job to stop them before they can hurt anyone in our town." It was a mantra that had steadied him before.

Vieintisiete

The cloud of dust got closer and closer. Luke watched with his telescope and could see that Billy Jones was out front. He also recognized several of the outlaws as wanted killers —he remembered them on back flyers. If all went well, the sheriff would do financially well on some of the large rewards offered by cattlemen's associations and states all the way from Montana to Idaho.

The outlaws rode directly into town and started shooting in every direction. Hooting in anticipation of the battle, they spurred their mounts into a shambling run that took them right down Main Street. Their firearms erupted into orange-white lances of flame. Powder odors and smoke wafted along the streets. The gunsels went right through the center of commerce, and then they wheeled their horses and started back for more destruction and carnage.

Several of the defenders started returning fire in a haphazard fashion and not being effective. Luke shouted at them to calm down and make their shots count. Luke chose his targets carefully, dropped a few outlaws, and then moved positions so that the gunsels wouldn't know where he was shooting from. In all the noise and confusion, he hadn't been able to line up Billy or the old bearded man, Leighton, in his sights.

The man next to him slumped over after a directed barrage from six of the outlaws. For some insane reason, he was hiding behind one-inch boards that any .38 or .44 caliber could penetrate, and most definitely a rifle slug. When dealing with these miscreants, Luke always kept in mind that many of them were war veterans, trained in the Civil War on both sides, and they knew about laying out directed fire. It looked like a rifle round took off the top of the man's right shoulder. He was howling in pain and giving away their location. Luke tore off the man's shirt and used it as direct pressure on the wound. He gave him a splinter of wood to chew on and try to absorb the pain. Luke reassured him that he would survive if he shut up and didn't take another round. Luke told him plain that he didn't calm down, the outlaws would hunt him down like a wounded animal and shoot him with a final round to the head.

The man realized the danger and muffled his crying as best he could. The bleeding slowed as his heart relaxed and reduced its pumping.

Luke moved again and took out another rider. He heard rapid gunfire near the banks. He knew that the deputy marshals were in the middle of a gunfight. He worried about them and their novice assistants, Tomas and Freddy.

Luke peeked through a break in the wooden wall. Two outlaws were charging the general store, probably to get more ammunition and firearms. The storekeeper, a fine man named Olaf Swenson, was defending the store through his glass window front. He took a round in the chest and he fell facedown onto the porch in front of the store. Luke knew that Olaf should never have exposed himself. Training would have taught him to let the attackers into the store and then shoot the bastards in the back. Olaf's wife came running out to her husband's dead body. Both outlaws mercilessly opened up on her with their pistols. She died instantly on top of her husband. Luke took careful aim and nailed one of the outlaws in the back of the head.

The other got away by running into the store. Luke couldn't get a second shot but he remembered the dirty blond hair sweeping out to a wide-brimmed cowboy hat. He would watch for that killer in the continuing melee.

Veintiocho

Wild Dog Larsen and his evil crew of five led the raid on the Arizona Trust Bank. Wild Dog had expected the bank to be a simple job of walking in, taking a few hostages and blasting those that resisted. He had heard the returning gunfire from other parts of the town but figured the bank would be a snap with a staff of unarmed citizens and maybe an old security guard that would try to be a hero and save other people's money.

Deputy Marshal Gutierrez ordered his men to clear the lobby of customers and wait for the outlaws to come in. Two of his deputies were pretending to be tellers but their handguns were laying on the counter rather than money.

Gutierrez said to Freddy, "You feel okay. Know what you're doing?"

"Yeah, I'm good. I'm ready!"

"Just stay calm and pick your targets. Often quick-fired shots go wild. Better to be precise and pick your targets, and if you do it right, your outlaw will go down. Then do the second shot to be sure." Then he added, "Don't get shot. Gregorio will get really pissed off if I let that happen."

"I won't get shot again. I know it. They haven't got me yet, and I won't let them hit me anymore."

Suddenly the door burst open, and Wild Dog came running in, and yelled out, "This is a robbery. Give us all your money and we won't hurt you." That must have been his standard spiel on previous jobs, but in this case he ran into an empty lobby. All the robbers had their guns out. Wild Dog shouted, "It's a trap. Pick your targets, boys."

The deputies were ready and commenced firing. They had already decided what they would do, but in that moment of hesitation and confusion, the outlaws lost their edge. They were also bunched up and made an easy target for several of the deputies that had shotguns. It was over in seconds. Two of the dying outlaws tried to raise their pistols from the floor and shoot but they were expeditiously given the *coupe de grace* by the deputies.

Gutierrez exclaimed, "Good job, amigos." He looked across the room and none of the deputies had been hit. But to his consternation, Freddy was bleeding from his forehead. Gutierrez said, "What the hell?"

Freddy said, "It's just a graze. I think a ricochet got me. I don't think I'll even need stitches."

"Thank goodness. I'd never hear the end of it from Gregorio." Gutierrez dabbed the wound with the first aid supplies at the bank. He said, "Yep, it's nothing. Not even sure if it counts as being shot. A coupla stitches will fix you right up."

Gutierrez then said, "Get all the guns and ammo from the dead guys, then stack up their bodies on the west wall against the window. The bodies will help us for barricades if we get rushed. Do not stick your heads outside. There may be sharpshooters waiting for a target.

Luke wanted us to stay here unless he or Carlos told us to move. Our post is secure."

The same scenario was happening as they spoke at the US Mutual Bank. The federal deputies and Tomas waited for the stupid outlaws to enter. Claude Russell led them in, again no resistance. It must be something taught at "dumb robber" school, because when the outlaws rushed in, Claude yelled out, "This is a hold-up! Give us your...."

Claude never managed to finish his sentence. He was almost cut in half with three shotgun blasts straight on, and the overspray from the shotgun loads managed to hit two more of the outlaws. The others went down trying to find a target. Again, it was over in seconds.

The experienced deputies gave the same instructions about getting the guns from the outlaws and stacking them against the windows. Again, they warned one another about exposing themselves near the windows. They weren't sure if Billy had posted sharpshooters on any of the targets.

Tomas got careless when he pulled one of the bodies to the window area. Although the windows had curtains, Tomas' body pushed the curtain aside and his side was exposed. A rifle shot was instantaneously fired, and the shot hit Tomas just below the heart. His eyes went wide for a fraction of a second, gasped, and he died and fell next to the dead outlaws.

Several guns opened up from outside the bank. The deputies went flat against the floor and told the bank employees to hide in the bullet-proof walk-in safe. Their experience told the deputies to lay low and not be peeking out the window corners for a target. They agreed if they were rushed, they would return deadly fire.

One of the deputies asserted, "I hope the bastards don't have dynamite. I would hate to be trapped here."

Several minutes later, several spaced disciplined rifles were fired, but not at the bank. The deputies knew return fire was coming from the defenders, maybe Luke and Gregorio and their snipers up on the roof tops.

"Not to worry about dynamite. I believe our snipers took them out before they could mount a charge from across the street."

The deputies picked up Tomas' body and moved him to the president's office. He was young and light, and never would have the chance to become a full-grown man. But he had the heart of a lion.

A terrible loss of a human being. Carlos would want immediate vengeance.

Veintinueve

Events were not going well for the outlaws. Leighton, Billy and Dirty Dick regrouped in a thick growth of trees near the boarding house. They each gave a report. The bank jobs had all gone bad. And to the best of what they had observed, the roof top snipers were taking a toll. Leighton was furious. So far they had only killed about five people and the outlaws had lost almost twenty riders. Riderless horses were running up and down the streets in total panic.

Dirty Dick said, "Forget the jail. The sheriff has that place barricaded and the doctor's office is the same way. The gawd-damn snipers are hitting us hard. They're on both sides of the main street. It's probably those 3Q owners. All seem good with their rifles."

Leighton said, "We never expected this kind of resistance from dirt farmers and cowboys. What do you boys suggest?"

Billy said, "Let's take the boarding house and we can get out of the firing ranges of their sniper rifles. Right now, they can keep picking us off. Maybe plan some more strategies. We have to find a safe place – right now, this town is not ready to give in."

Dirty Dick said, "I like the plan. Looks like the front is barricaded but when I rode around back, it looked empty. Doesn't seem to be any protection."

"Let's go. Bring along a couple of the boys to watch our backs.'

Leighton and his crew displayed no finesse or advance planning. They just went to the back and haphazardly busted down the doors. Perro and his two dog friends started howling and of course, Perro went for the first intruder. The other dogs followed suit. They were easily kicked off, but Perro attacked and clamped his jaws on the first intruder, which he decided to release and then tried for the neck. Leighton tried to shoot the dog but his shot went wild and hit one of the outlaws in the right shoulder. Two outlaws were now incapitated.

After telling Doc, Carmen and Joanna to watch the front, Abby and Alyce responded to the back door. The outlaws were inside now. Billy found a hammer and tried beating Perro off the outlaw. After being struck a dozen times, Perro released his grip and fell to the floor.

When Leighton saw Abby, he raised his eyebrows in surprise and said, "You're the one. I'll have you now."

Abby exploded in rage when she remembered that it was Leighton's goons that had raped and nearly killed Joanna. She rocked back on her feet to gain distance so he couldn't grab her or her revolver. Her thumb raked the hammer on her Bisley Colt as Leighton was cocking his revolver and extending his elbow to deliver a deadly shot to her chest. Abby's shot went first, striking him on the upper thigh with her 250 grain slug that slammed him hard and ruined his aim. His shot went through her blouse.

With a quick shift of her weight and trying to keep Leighton between her and the other gunsels, she delivered a strong kick to his thigh that dropped him to his knees. Alyce had entered the fray and fired at the group with her revolver. Leighton regained his composure and sent another shot at Abby, this time catching her in the abdomen at a deadly angle. She managed to stroke the trigger of her revolver, and fire and lead erupted from the muzzle. The lump of lead made a meaty, smacking sound. Through the halo of smoke from the guns firing in a small space, Abby's last visions were of Leighton's head jerking and him falling next to her.

Alyce got a clear shot with her scattergun, and one of the wounded outlaws yelled, "Let's get out of here. This whole raid has gone wrong."

Carlos and Hussong responded to the scene as the outlaws were riding roughshod out of town. Carlos made a snap shot with his carbine and caught Dirty Dick dead center in the back. Luke and Gregorio and their fellow snipers had heard the shots coming from the boarding house and made their way over the rooftops. Gregorio spotted several of the outlaws riding like blazes to leave town. He took careful aim resting his rifle on a brick wall for support. He dropped two *ladrones* from their horses with two shots. They wouldn't be robbing or terrorizing any more western towns.

As Luke was dropping to the ground from his roof top, he noticed a blonde long haired outlaw, wearing a large black hat, slipping through the store alleys, searching for a way out of town. The outlaw was definitely the man responsible for the couple's deaths at the general store. Luke drew a lethal bead on him and at the last minute, realized it was the lawman's code that the judge and jury should decide the guilt and sentence of the criminal. He was no longer threatened. It wasn't self-defense and it was his job to take the lawbreakers to court, and let the court process them. He dropped the sights of the rifle for a lower shot. He was too tired and didn't feel like a fistfight after a long foot pursuit, so he shot the *pendejo* in the legs. The man cried out in excruciating pain. Luke asked two of his fellow snipers to get the man down to the jail and leave him with Sheriff Mortimer. He had no idea when Doc could respond.

When Gregorio walked into the back of the boarding house, he saw two wounded outlaws tied up and the old bearded man dead.

Doc was working on someone, and Alyce was crying. He looked closer and saw the victim was Abby. She had lost too much blood but she was still alive. Gregorio looked into her face and she faintly smiled. She barely murmured, "We stopped them. Tell Joanna we got the bastard that hurt her."

Gregorio said, "Save your strength. We gotta get you better and back on the stagecoach."

"Not going to happen, *mi vaquero*. I am very cold."

"I love you."

"I know. *Tu amo, Corazon.*"

Abby passed while gently cradled in Gregorio's arms. It seemed surreal to see a macho man like Gregorio, tears flowing and holding onto something dear. But Gregorio had fallen totally in love on the first day he saw her driving the stagecoach.

Doc told Luke, "It was a nasty bad luck shot. Leighton had shot upwards, and the bullet went through several vital organs and likely nicked the heart sack. The finest hospital in Chicago couldn't have saved her.

Doc and Luke walked into the front parlor and saw that Carmen and Joanna were still holding their post in protecting the front door and windows. Luke said, "It's over, ladies. You were wonderful. Now go help Alyce with Abby. We're afraid that she's been killed by Leighton."

Carmen spit out, "*Puerco.* The man is a pig!"

Joanna said, "Poor Abby. Gregorio loved her so."

The women did what they had to do.

Luke went to the pantry and found Jesus safe but shaking. He re-assured the lad that everything was now okay. Jesus had seen too much tragedy in his short life.

Perro was still struggling to live. Even close to death after so many hammer blows, he looked up adoringly with his silver-gold eyes. He blinked several times and died. Luke patted him on the chest with tenderness, and said, "Goodbye my friend." Jesus patted him too – they had already formed a bond.

Treinta

As the defenders broke cover, Carlos learned from the deputy marshals that the outlaws had killed his brother, Tomas. Carlos flushed bright red and his body tensed. He mumbled something about telling his mother. She had frail health.

Both he and Luke made a quick inventory of the dead outlaws and couldn't find Billy. They had killed all the leaders and most of the outlaws, but they wanted crazy Billy Jones. After learning that there were two wounded outlaws at the boarding house, he ran to the back door and found them tied up with their backs against the wall.

Carlos approached the outlaws and asked where Billy would be heading and what was he riding. The first man made an irretrievable big-mistake answer when he said, "I don't know nothing, greaser. I don't have to talk to you. I know my rights. I'm a white man."

"Last chance before I shoot you between the eyes."

"You wouldn't dare with all these witnesses."

"You're right. He then kicked the first one on his wounded side, and then kicked the knee of the outlaw with the leg wound." They screamed in pain and yelled for the sheriff to come help them. The sheriff was busy rounding up dead bodies off the street.

Gregorio joined them and said he would glad to help and he asked the men to be reasonable and answer Carlos' questions. Human emotion was at the apex of anger. Carlos had lost a brother and Gregorio his lover and future wife.

The first outlaw said, "We don't have to talk to you either. You look like another greaser."

Gregorio began kicking them both with his sharp-pointed riding boots. After several good hits, Alyce said. "Don't kill these idiots. We want to save them for the hangmen." They were bleeding and withering in pain but decided to stay alive. In their feeble little minds, they were thinking that there might a chance of escape and avoiding the hangman.

The first outlaw said, "We don't owe Billy anything. He's a real nut case. He's more ruthless than Leighton."

"Tell us where to find him. What color of horse does he ride?"

"Billy has a little shack up near Casa Grande. He likes to take his women up there. Vicky at Leighton's brothel used to get pissed at him because often he would take a whore up there, and she wouldn't make it back for work. Several of the girls were popular and brought a lot of money into Vicky's coffers, especially on paydays. Billy boasted to several of the guys that he had tortured the girls and then killed them, dumping their bodies in the desert for the coyotes."

"Why Casa Grande? And how about his horse?"

"Casa Grande has plenty of water and some protected canyons. You can see for miles if anyone tries to make an approach to the cabin. He usually rides a gelded paint, a strong horse he cheated off some sucker in a poker game. You best watch Billy. He's a devious, tricky fellow – can't be trusted. He probably has three or four other outlaws with him. The guys are worried about Billy's moods and temper, but they also know he's good at killing and thieving. With Billy, you never have to go broke, or without girls."

Carlos, Gregorio and Luke agreed to meet in one hour and be ready for the chase after Billy. Before he left, he and Alyce found Perro and wrapped him in a warm wool blanket and carried out back of the boarding house for a burial spot near his favorite tree. Joanna's two dogs followed and made small screeching sounds like small babies. Luke said a few words about Perro being a good friend and how he had saved him so many times. Luke promised that he would settle the score.

Alyce hugged him and she helped him pack for his journey. She knew there was no stopping the three men from their mission. She said, "Go do what you must. Joanna, Carmen and I will take care of things here. Doc has gone to help the sheriff with a couple of defenders that had minor injuries."

They hugged. She ordered, "You get back safe. You've got me waiting, and two children to raise."

"I will be back!"

Hussong had seen a lone warrior on a knoll just outside the city limits. He waved at the brave, and the man made a gesture to join him. So he did.

The three men rode out just before dark. The moon was still full and they planned traveling for a few hours and then making camp. Luke thought it strange that they couldn't find Hussong. He would have made the perfect guide to Casa Grande but Carlos said he could find the way simply from following the old stagecoach road and by talking to pilgrims along the way.

Luke had seen Hussong in battle. He was aggressive but careful, and managed to kill a few outlaws with his long knives. He was hoping that Hussong hadn't been injured and gone off to the Hopi plateaus.

They became philosophical around the fire, talking about life, their loves and what their future plans were. Luke got serious and said, "We have to plan a field of fire, so we don't shoot each other."

Gregorio smiled said, "We've heard this before. You take the left, I'll take the right, and I suppose, you Carlos, will be the center shooter."

"Makes me no difference. I just want a clear shot at the bastard."

Next morning, there was a note on Luke's saddle, just a few feet from his bedroll where he had been sleeping. It said, "I am with you along the way. Do not worry." It was signed "H."

He showed the note to his compatriots, and said, "This is when I miss Perro. No one could get close to me because of that dog. I glad it was Hussong out there, and not a wild renegade Apache."

Carlos said, "I can cover you. My hearing is still sharp. I saw him come in. I was just watching if he was a threat. I didn't make a sound."

Luke said, "Let's finish breakfast and coffee, and get on the move. I think we can make it almost to Casa Grande tonight if we push hard. Then we can reconnoiter and figure out our best move."

Gregorio asserted, "Hopefully that crazy Billy hasn't gone to Phoenix. In his own stupid mind, he might figure he'll just take over Leighton's empire. It will be harder to catch him there. Phoenix is so gigantic compared to Tucson."

At one of their rest stops, the sudden secession of insect noise and the absence of all birdcalls alerted them to as yet an undisclosed danger. Being experienced hands, they knew to stay alive in the wilderness you had to be able to see and hear the unordinary. As they started to move again nearing a ridge, they stopped and listened. Barely, they heard the distinctive calls of the meadowlarks and the screech of a hawk on the hunt.

On a bluff above them, Carlos saw what he believed to a horse or some other type of movement. But then it was gone in a flash. He said, "Probably a deer but there's something going on around us. I feel like we're being watched."

Luke said, "Stay sharp. Keep your guns ready. This is definitely Indian country, and sometimes raiders come up from Mexico."

At sunset, they reached the boundaries of Casa Grande and set up camp. Carlos spoke to nearby farmers, and learned that Billy and his criminal brethren had been spotted near his cabin. The farmer told him how to approach without being seen. It involved a mountain climb for about three miles.

Luke said, "Damn, I hope my old knees hold up."

Carlos laughed and said, "It's either that or a frontal assault facing their rifles."

"My knees will just have to suffer."

The three men went to bed early, slept off and on, and started to rise during the false dawn. Luke thought it strange that he smelled coffee. Carlos and Gregorio were still in their bedrolls. A voice said, "Time to rise and shine. The bacon will be ready in ten minutes." Hussong handed Luke a cup of fresh, steaming coffee.

"How in the hell did you get into our camp? Are you going to guide us to Billy's cabin?"

"Nope!"

"Why not?"

"Billy and three of his gunsels left last night for Phoenix."

"How do you know all this stuff?"

"Good eyes and informants. Many of these people in this valley are a mixture of different tribes, and a lot of Mexicans. The Mexicans are descended from Spanish soldiers who settled here and intermingled with the various tribes. It's kind of a neutral zone and everyone seems to get along. They talked to me freely. They have seen the cruelty of Billy and his *malo* friends. Farmers have found several female bodies where Billy dumped them in the desert. The women looked like they had been savagely beaten, and then died from knife wounds. Two of the women had bite marks. It wasn't clear if Billy had done that or wild animals bit them after the bodies were left to rot."

Carlos and Gregorio were up and about, and sharing the coffee. The bacon and eggs were ready in minutes. Luke took out and shared a package of sweet rolls that Alyce had packed for him.

"Luke, what do you think we ought to do? I want that gawd-damn Billy to pay!"

"I think we should go to town and grab Billy for trial in Tucson. Gregorio and I will go to the Emporium Building and get a feel of what's going on. I'm sure there's a real power struggle between Leighton's lieutenants."

Carlos and Gregorio looked at each other, and silently thought, "Trial? There ain't going to be any trial."

Gregorio said, "That jerk knows us. What good can we do if he spots us? What if he rounds up some help?"

"I see that as an opportunity to save the Arizona taxpayers a lot of money. We'll just blast him on the spot and mark the case "closed."

Hussong said, "He's liable to be loaded down with more outlaws and guns."

Carlos added, "Yeah, but most of those gunslingers would like to see Billy gone. They might even help us."

Luke chuckled, "That part of it is true."

"We'll finish breakfast and be on our way. It's a good morning for a gunfight."

Within two hours, they were tying up their horses in front of the Emporium. Carlos and Hussong went to the restaurant across from the Emporium where they could see a good view of the front door. Luke and Gregorio entered and walked over to the bar and business reception area. The bar area was full of ne'er-do-wells and a motley crew of misfits, probably all waiting for a job with Leighton. Luke thought it would be fun to walk through the bar wearing his deputy marshal badge and carrying a thick file of "wanted flyers," and timing how fast the bar would empty.

A portly, somber-looking man with huge sideburns approached them. His long graying hair hung straight down on his shoulders, and fit the image of a bookish type of accountant. His skin was sickly white. His suit was stained.

He slightly bowed his head and introduced himself as Robinson Burton. He had his thumb hooked in his red brocade vest and he appeared full of himself, a lot of fluff but little substance. He said, in a cockney English accent, "I am the hotel and bar manager. May I inquire of your business? You look like you've been on the trail for many days."

Luke answered, "No you can't inquire Burton. We want to talk to Timothy Leighton and right now. He cheated us out of a hundred cows and also two of my prize bulls."

"Well, Mr. Leighton is away on business. Maybe I can help you."

"No, that won't do. You look like you haven't been in the sun in your entire life. Maybe we can talk to a couple of his cowboys, Billy Jones and Dirty Dick. Those guys know what happened to our cows."

"That barbarian Dirty Dick is also out of town on some special assignment. He's a mean man, that one. He likes to mimic my British accent. He might have gone to Tucson or Mexico."

"And Billy?"

"He came in yesterday. I'm not sure where he is or what he is doing. He may well be in Leighton's business suite. I believe he had an appointment with Mr. Leighton's personal secretary, Benjamin."

Luke asked, "Is Billy trying to take over everything?"

"He always is. He's Mr. Leighton's weak spot. None of us can understand why he keeps Billy on the payroll."

Luke thought to himself, "He keeps him around to take care of "details," like someone who needs to disappear or a stubborn rancher to assassinate, or someone that cheats on the receipts from the bar.."

Gregorio demanded, "Take us to Leighton's suite. We want to talk to Billy."

"Sorry, I can't do that. It is against the rules."

"Burton, I don't have time to follow your ridiculous rules. Now take me to the suite or I will cut off your balls. You understand?"

Burton was real prissy and answered, "And I will call security and you will be thrown out on your butt."

Gregorio slipped in behind Burton, pushed a knife against his ribs, and said, "You will die before you can yell for help. Now get moving to the stairway. Don't bullshit us! We know his suite is on the third floor."

They followed Burton to the stairway and walked to the third floor. Burton knocked on the door, dreading the dressing-down he would get from Benjamin. He was hoping Billy wasn't there. Billy would even be worse and insult him in front of everyone. No one answered.

Luke tried the door. It was locked. He asked Burton if he had a key. He replied in the negative. Gregorio said, "Stand back. I am going to use my personal size 11 key." The door gave way on the first kick.

Guns drawn, the men entered the room expecting Billy might be hiding inside.

Burton tried to run away, but Gregorio held him by the arm. The side window to the fire escape was open. When they look into the side secretary office, they observed Benjamin slumped over his desk. His face was lying in a pool of blood. Luke raised his head by pulling on his hair. He had been shot in the center of his forehead, and the bullet had exited at the back of his skull. He was dead.

The men heard the vibrating fire escape, like someone was taking two to three steps at a time. Luke told Gregorio to chase him down the metal stairway, and he would run to the bottom inside, and try and nab him below.

Burton asked, "What should I do?"

"Call the sheriff for starters. You got a dead guy in your building."

"Was that Billy on the stairway? I know he hated Benjamin."

"We don't know. The guy was running full-out. All we saw was the back of his head."

Treinta Y Uno

When Luke met up with Gregorio at the bottom of the fire escape, he told him that the possible killer had escaped into the heart of the commercial center. It was market day and there were thousands of people milling about, buying vegetables and meats, and new clothes and supplies for the ranches and farms. They hadn't got a good look at him – he was Billy's body size but they weren't sure it was him.

Word travels fast in town squares. A man walked over to Luke and Gregorio and said to Luke, "Are you a deputy marshal? I saw you talking to Marshal O'Reilly one afternoon at a restaurant."

"Could be. And you are?"

"My name is Jed Washington. I used to own a small ranch north of Phoenix until Leighton ran me off and threatened my wife and children."

"Sorry about that, but why are you talking to us?"

"First, that fellow you were chasing is Billy Jones, a ruthless bag of shit. And second, I know where he'll be hiding."

They talked more in length. Luke got a good feeling about Jed, a black man, stocky and barrel-chested, who gave off an aura of reliability. He had a brooding quiet demeanor about him that spoke of suppressed violence, the kind that could erupt if provoked. It was probably good that he didn't blow up at Leighton or he would be dead by now, including his family. His voice was confident and melodic.

Gregorio asked him a few questions and was watching his body language. Luke could tell that Gregorio was accepting Jed as to who he said he was, and not as another outlaw setting them up for an ambush or sending them on a false goose chase. Hussong and Carlos had joined them.

Luke said, "Hussong, I want you to go find Marshal Gus O'Reilly and bring back several of his deputies. Deputy Gutierrez should be back in Phoenix by now. If the Marshal asks why we need him just tell him we're going after a federal fugitive."

"Should we meet at the restaurant cross the street? Their Mexican food is the best."

"Appears to be a good spot. We can have a meal and get stronger while you're rounding up the federal officers."

When they heard a commotion on the street, they looked through the restaurant windows and saw the local sheriff and three of his deputies conversing with Burton at the front door of the Emporium. It was murder investigation time. The 3Q bunch knew they had to find Billy before the local officers so they could transport his sorry ass back to Tucson.

The feds showed up in thirty minutes and Jed guided them to Billy's town hideout. They stayed in the shadows and watched the small house for several minutes. There wasn't much movement, a few birds and a snorting horse. Luke and Gregorio scanned all the rooftops and hiding places in the trees. Luke said, "It looks okay to move."

Jed stated, "Billy is in there. My friend followed him after he ran down the fire escape."

"Are you sure that you friend isn't in cahoots with the outlaws, like being paid as an informant. He wouldn't set us for an ambush, would he?"

"Nope. He hates those people. They also took his little farm, and raped his wife while they were at it."

Luke asked, "Do you have a suggestion, Marshal?"

"No, I'll let Gutierrez handle our part of it." O'Reilly appeared nervous wringing his hands. This could all go wrong for his political career.

"Okay, here what I suggest. You federals cover the back and snag the rats as they scurry out to escape."

"We'll kick in the front door and surprise the hell out of them. Shoot if you have to but try to keep Billy alive. We want him for trial in Tucson."

Carlos again glanced at Gregorio. Their expressions were subtle but meaningful.

The plan was fast and efficient. There were five outlaws inside. Everyone had been drinking and were mostly passed out from alcohol Three of the outlaws managed to sneak out the back with guns in hand. They saw the federal deputies and started firing. That was their last stupid decision on earth. They were all dead in seconds. Luke and Hussong caught one outlaw in bed with a female, and they were quickly subdued. Gregorio and Carlos found Billy sound asleep in bed, and when he tried to jump through a window, they pulled him back inside and Gregorio knocked him unconscious with his shotgun butt.

Gregorio said to Carlos, "If he starts to move, kick him in the head."

"Good job, men. Deputy Gutierrez has told me that he will clean up this mess and write the reports. He'll take care of the one outlaw that survived and also the female. He remembered her from a federal flyer – apparently she's wanted in Colorado for rolling drunks. We need to start riding for Tucson with Billy before the sheriff ambles over our way."

Carlos said, "Good thing we ate platefuls of that good Mexican chow. The food in our saddlebags is about gone."

Gregorio said, "We'll probably get darn hungry on the way back."

Hussong said, "You won't have to worry about that." Luke just figured they'd do some hunting on the way back. As much as he enjoyed deer and quail, he was looking forward to having a juicy beef steak in Tucson.

Hussong and Carlos had rounded up the horses and they were ready to ride. They had found Billy's paint in the back yard. The outlaws' other horses were turned loose. Gutierrez said he didn't have anywhere to stable the mounts.

The men made it back safely to their old camp in Casa Grande. Billy's hands had been tied all day to his saddle horn. He complained and sniveled the whole way but quieted temporarily each time when Carlos or Gregorio slapped him on the back of his head with their reins.

When they reached a suitable camping spot, Billy was tied to a tree and wasn't able to move about. The men had already decided Billy was a major escape risk and kept him incapacitated and secure. There was no chance that he could grab a gun or knife. Carlos did untie one hand when they let him eat and drink but checked him closely when they retied him.

When he asked to answer nature's call, Carlos told him, "Piss in your pants. We're not taking you anywhere."

Luke made assignments for the night's watch. They weren't expecting trouble but again Carlos had seen a quick passing shadow along the trail. It was too far north for Geronimo's Apaches. It was felt by all the men that Billy's outlaw pals wouldn't be trying to set him free. Hussong volunteered to take the four o'clock assignment in the early morning.

The night passed quietly. Billy complained several times that he was hungry and then he couldn't sleep because his ropes were too tight. No one paid him any mind.

Dawn broke and Luke decided it was time to start moving. He sat up, and said to the other men, "Daylight is wasting. Let's get some coffee." He noticed that Billy was asleep and still bound tightly. He didn't immediately see Hussong. The other men sat up and were dreadfully startled when they saw twenty Apache braves sitting quietly and watching their every move. The braves were wearing their war paint but their rifles were at their sides, non-threatening. The men reached for their firearms and found them gone.

Hussong stepped forward from behind the group. He said, "I have all your guns. These braves do not intend to hurt you, and I didn't want a shootout to erupt."

"Shit, we're outnumbered and outgunned. What's happening here?" After seeing that everyone was calm and relaxed, Luke smiled and said, "Did you bring us breakfast? Last time you surprised us like this you had the coffee ready."

"No coffee now. Will boil up some later." He paused and asserted, "The warriors only want one thing – Billy Jones. They are here to take him back to their village."

"Hussong, that's not going to happen. He's a federal prisoner and I'm taking him back to Tucson for trial."

Billy had awakened, and was wailing and trembling out of fear. "Marshal, you can't let them take me!" He was ignored.

Hussong answered, "Luke, they say that he's going with them. They want him for Indian retribution."

A small Apache dressed in male attire stepped forward. She had a high, feminine voice. She said, "I am Flower Petal. He is mine to take back. He killed my family members at the 3Q Ranch. He's going to pay the price and no one can stop me. Geronimo told us that this is my decision." She looked over at the older warrior, "Magic Tree, please tell him this is true."

Magic Tree said, "What Flower Petal says is what Geronimo decided. He sent us with her to settle the score. We have been following you for several days. We waited until you left Phoenix." Three warriors stepped forward with large knives and walked towards the prisoner.

Billy blurted out in a pleading voice, "Marshal, you can't let them kill me. It's your job to take care of me." Luke moved in front of Billy trying to protect his prisoner. Gregorio and Carlos sensed a confrontation developing and they took Luke by the arms and pulled him back. He made a halfway effort to resist.

Gregorio said, "I want to see him have a trial and then hang the son-of-a-bitch. But this is better. Justice will be served for us all. The Almighty has his own way of handling these situations. Remember in the Bible about 'an eye for eye?' That's what is happening here."

Gregorio and Carlos felt Luke's muscles lose their tension.

The three warriors cut the ropes from Billy and moved him to a horse. Magic Tree said, "Your report should say that he was forcefully taken from you. The white man's government is already angry with us. Another complaint will not matter."

Gregorio looked Billy square in the face and said, "Adios, Muchacho! You bastards killed my Abby. Burn in hell!"

"No, it's all a mistake. The other guys did it. Please save me. You let me go before!"

"No more!"

Billy struggled but he was struck a sound blow by a war club. He was barely conscious and the warriors placed him on his saddle and tied him. They gagged him so he would stop yelling and begging for his life.

Luke asked, "What will happen now?"

Flower Petal answered, "It is not your worry. I will turn him over to the females of my tribe to determine his fate. You will never see him again."

Carlos said, "Ouch! *Madre de Dios!*"

Hussong exclaimed, "Ai-yee!"

Magic Tree managed a smile. He said, "And it will be slow. The women will tie him to a stake in the middle of the village, and many will beat him with switches as they pass by. The women do not rush, and they have many sharp knives for the finish. They will remove his manhood."

Carlos said, "A dull knife would be better."

Gregorio thought himself, "I would like to see it happen."

Luke said to Gregorio, "We have a legal term for this whole situation *quid pro quo*, meaning things even out, tit for tat. Justice is served."

Gregorio grinned and said, "You're right but I would still like to be there when he's released to the women." Gregorio turned away and mumbled, "For what he did to Abby."

Before the Apaches rode off, Luke spoke privately to Flower Petal about adopting Jesus and that his wife-to-be was Navajo. She said, "I saw your Hopi friend, Hussong, save him. To me, it was a spiritual omen that the boy would be in good hands. It is right that you be giving him a new life. Tell the Navajo-woman to be a good mother."

"It will be so. Thank you."

As the Apaches rode off, Luke said, "Hussong, I'll trade you a painted horse for a strong cup of coffee. Billy won't be needing either."

"That's a fine horse. You're not angry with me?"

Luke shook his hand and said, "The level of my anger will depend on how good your coffee is."

La Conclusion

It was along slow walk to the cemetery on top of the knoll that allowed a beautiful view of the valleys in very direction. The town had held the bodies in the ice house until the men got back from Phoenix. The use of the freight wagon carrying the bodies was donated from one of Abby's friends. The man volunteered to drive the wagon. The appreciative townsmen had dug the graves the night before. The coroner's carpenters had prepared the coffins. The remaining 3Q members still alive and the sheriff's deputies were the pallbearers. It was very pleasant day for Arizona. The birds were singing their daily songs, the earth continued to spin on its axis, and the nearby trees were swaying in the gentle breeze. It was all so eternal, and indicative that life goes on. A lone eagle watched them from hundreds of feet high in the ever-changing sky of *azul.* A chuckwalla spotted the eagle's flight and headed for cover.

The priest at the church service discussed the value of the two friends being committed to God's care. He talked of their histories and life's experiences and how they had served mankind in the pursuit of safety and the welfare of their friends and neighbors. They were both brave people who had died fighting against tyranny and the deeds of the devil. Gregorio sat with Luke and Alyce on one side and on the other side was Carlos. He was openly crying and holding his crucifix.

The parish priest said the words that affect every human being eventually. He said in a strong, clear voice, "Dust thou art and unto dust shalt thou return. Ashes to ashes, dust to dust, in the clear and certain hope of the resurrection, we commit the bodies of our brother Tomas and sister Abby to the earth until our Lord comes again in glory. In the name of the Father, and of the Son, and of the Holy Ghost..."

He continued, "And in a moment of silence, please say your private prayer for our beloved, Abby Hawkins, and Tomas Rivera. They have gone to stay with Jesus forever and forever." The minute passed with an "Amen" from the priest and from the friends and family. They filed past the graves and dropped flowers on the caskets in the burial sites. On the gentle slopes back to town, Carmen calmly said to Gregorio, "When I die, I want to be buried next to my husband, Jesse Quinn, on the hilltop next to the cabin. It is so peaceful there."

"*Madre*, don't leave too soon I pray."

As they left the cemetery, friends and family remembered the lives of their loved ones and how they had bravely fought for freedom and showed no fear in the face of adversity. They were the pioneer stock of the Old West and would continue to be the heart and soul of future generations.

The 3Q Ranch had lost two of its original owners, Gabe and Tomas, and another potential member that would have probably been joining them in ownership, Abby. Fortunately the lawyer had worked out the details, adjustments had been made, and the new changes were entered into the court record. Luke also explained that new owners might be added to his section, like Alyce, Jesus and Margarita, if all went well.

Sheriff Mortimer had finished his inventory. A total of five defenders and thirty-two outlaws were killed. The five defenders were given Christian funerals by their families. It was discussed hot and heavy in city council meetings as to what do with the outlaw bodies. By the third day, the sheriff told them that something had to be done because the bodies were contaminated, rotting and becoming smelly. Finally the council voted that the sheriff record what information was available about the deceased, and then build a huge funeral pyre. One of the council members said, "Our citizens don't want them in our municipal cemetery. The only answer is to make a pile of old lumber and tree branches, and return the outlaws to the soil. That's what they do in Oriental countries. That makes a lot of sense to me and solves our dead body problem." He made a motion and it passed unanimously.

Ten of the miscreants were recovering from their injuries in the jailhouse. Their trials would be coming up when the circuit judge dropped by. About ten of the outlaws escaped. The sheriff wasn't sure of the exact numbers – no one was. Twelve of the dead and captured outlaws were wanted in other jurisdictions, so the sheriff ended up with over ten thousand dollars in bounty. He shared this with his deputies, including the four reservists. Federal deputies were prohibited by law and regulations for receiving rewards for wanted prisoners.

Life went on in Tucson, and businesses now prospered out from under the dark veil of tyranny and uncertainty. Olaf's brother from Minnesota came to town and reopened the general store. He placed a plaque on the outside wall of the store in Olaf and his wife's memory.

When it seemed appropriate several months later, Luke proposed to Alyce with the proviso that they determine if her husband was still alive, and if so, did she want to return to him and if not, seek a divorce in the white man's courts. She accepted his proposal with only one requirement, that since Flower Petal said Jesus could live with Alyce, that the boy be officially adopted on their wedding day.

Luke laughingly said, "You mean our boy, Jesus Jesse Quinn? I had to put my father's name in there somewhere."

"Won't be hard to figure out his new nickname, Little JJ."

"You got it. Where is that tiny tyke, our Apache-Navajo-American boy?"

"Where do your think? He's out with Hussong, learning to hunt and fish."

"Makes sense to me. My old knees aren't so good at climbing mountains or crossing the slippery rocks in the streams."

She slyly asked, "Are they any good in the bedroom?"

"Only one way to find out, my little Indian maiden."

Next day, the search began for Alyce's husband, Iron Eyes. Alyce checked all her Indian sources, relatives, friends and the chiefs and Indian agents on the Navajo reservation. Luke asked Marshal Gus O'Reilly and Deputy Gutierrez, and the local sheriff Charley Mortimer. All telegraph inquiries and searches had negative returns.

Luke and Hussong headed for the San Carlos reservation. Geronimo had already surrendered and was on a supervised train ride to Florida. But the medicine man and the local chief remembered Iron Eyes. He said that there had been a dispute several years before over lands bordering the Navajo and Apache Reservations. Iron Eyes fought hard when the Apaches moved their stock onto the Navajo Reservation. A two-day mobile fight ensued on land between the desert floor and the red rock mountains. It was not a battle of sniping and sneaking in the night – it was a battle fought man-to-man in daylight. Iron Eyes charged straight-on to two Apache warriors. He killed one but was then was shot fatally by the second warrior. He fought hard and bravely.

According to the surviving brave, his last words were enigmatic. He could have been talking about his wife or daughter when he said, "Say goodbye for me. She is so beautiful." Because he fought strongly and without fear, the Apaches conducted a warrior ceremony for him, and then returned his body to the Navajos. As a result, the tribes reached an agreement about the land for grazing and hunting. His body was left high in a chimney of the red rocks, protected from wild beasts and the elements. JJ would grow up knowing that his biological father was a respected warrior of the highest degree.

Luke and Hussong spotted Flower Petal in the center of the populated portion of the Apache reservation. She had resumed her female appearance and was making beaded necklaces in a circle of women. She looked happy and fulfilled. She saw them and raised her eyebrows in acknowledgement. Her hair had grown long again. It was speckled with gray, but her face looked relaxed and soft. She stood and brought them a drink and several pieces of cactus candy, and said in broken English, "Thank you for helping me. My soul is now content." She gave them handsome jewelry to wear personally for men, and a turquoise wedding necklace for Alyce. The silver smithing was magnificent.

No mention of Billy Jones was made.

With the Iron Eyes mystery settled, Luke and Alyce planned their wedding day for the upcoming weekend. The adoption paperwork had already been done for JJ. He was the wedding ring bearer and one of Joanna's nieces carried the flowers. Alyce's mother, Blue Butterfly, and her daughter, Margarita, rode in from the reservation for the ceremony.

Luke was amused when he saw a lone rider on an old mule coming in behind the ladies. It was Rafael, still alive and now very tanned and fit. The Navajos kept him in only a pair of shorts and allowed him only to leave his hut when he was working; and they gave him plenty to do from chopping wood to irrigating the corn fields. He had not tried to escape even when the elders told him that he could go at any time, and in any direction. They explained that if the dry desert didn't kill him, some of the neighboring tribes might. He was worried about the bloodthirsty Apaches, and he had no idea that peace has been made between the longtime adversaries. He still had his five dollar coin. Carlos took him to the train station and bought him a one-way ticket to Denver. He asked no questions about Leighton and his grand plans.

For the big wedding, Luke arranged for a preacher and an organist. The ceremony was in a non-denomination church on the outskirts of town near a gentle stream with giant oak trees. The preacher and his wife also conducted a school for elementary-level youngsters during the week. The inside walls of the old white clapboard building were covered with arithmetic problems, student drawings, and essays on finding peace in Arizona. The preacher refused his normal fee, saying "Luke, how could we charge you? Your friends saved our church from burning to the ground."

The narrow dual-purpose church was filled with invited guests, and loads of well-wishers were outside trying to stay in the shade while the sun beat down. Standing at the altar was the good Reverend Henry Doolittle, Maid of Honor Joanna Carson and Best Man Gregorio Isaacs. As planned, the ceremony was short and sweet.

Reverend Doolittle asked, "Do you, Luke, take this woman, Alyce, to be your lawful wedded wife? To love, honor and cherish her, for richer or poorer, in sickness and health for so long as you both live?"

"I definitely do," Luke broadcast in a loud, clear voice.

"And do you, Alyce, take this man, Luke to be your lawful wedded husband? To love, honor and obey, through sickness and health, for richer or poorer, until death you do part?"

"I do," Alyce calmly answered, eyes sparkling with promise and excitement. She was over-flowing and beaming with love.

"Then, by the power vested in me by God Almighty and with the authority of the Territory of Arizona, I now pronounce you man and wife. You may kiss the bride, Luke."

Happily, the couple embraced, and he kissed her with deep emotion. The audience clapped. A tired, beat-up wheezing pump organ began the Mendelssohn wedding recessional and as the couple walked down the aisle, the audience followed them out of the church. Rice and flowers flew, and the hungry squirrels watched from a nearby tree, ready for a free meal of rice. Several men fired off their handguns in a safe direction and shouted in celebration. The boys and girls ran in delight, just being loose to escape the adult world of sitting quiet. JJ and Margarita became immediate friends. There was enough age difference that Margarita would always be the "big sister" and not challenged for everything she said.

The church ladies had organized a western-style buffet and soon plates were being filled with potato salad, pickled beets, hot jalapeno peppers, and sliced beef. The whole-wheat bread was fresh from the bakery. A band of guitars, banjos, and makeshift drums, and a lone fiddle was knocking out a series of well-known and dancing songs. After a quick bite, the children were now climbing the trees, and irritating the hell out of the squirrels and feathered creatures, especially four squawky blackbirds.

The happy couple shook hands with the parishioners and hugged their friends and family. It was festive and carefree, and it was an event that one would wish that time stood still, and that the moment would never end.

Luke saw Gregorio sitting by himself near the back of the church. He squeezed Alyce's hand and said, "I've got to go talk to Gregorio. This must a very sad day for him."

"Take him some tequila and a cigar."

Luke looked at her in bewilderment, "Did you say tequila?"

"Yeah, the gunfights are over for now. No worries now about your reflexes and your aim. Tequila shots are part of male bonding, sitting around a fire and talking "story." But I could never could understand why you guys like sucking on old tobacco joints. Did you miss out on your mama's teats?"

"Oh no, my mother had wonderful breasts."

"Sucking is woman's work, unless...." She chuckled.

He laughed and said, "Nope, you know that's not my preference. Maybe cigars just taste good."

"Whatever the case, enjoy being with your brother, Gregorio. Spruce him up – we'll do our best to get him over Abby."

"We'll visit Hussong and Carlos tomorrow. They have gone to the mountains to meditate, and visit Tomas in the spiritual world."

Luke continued, "They said they had a surprise for us. What's that all about?"

"Our friends set us up a cozy tent with piles of blankets and pillows on a nearby ridge for our honeymoon. The moon is almost full, and it will be a bright night. Hussong has promised not to spy."

While Alyce chatted with her friends and introduced Margarita to everyone, Luke sat and supported Gregorio. There wasn't much that could be said that hadn't been spoken of, so they had their tequila and Mexican cigars. Luke said, "You've been great in all this, you know. I am very pleased that we will be ranching together."

Gregorio looked off to the mountains and the fluffy white cumulus clouds leaning against the highest peaks. He was silent. His eyes were moist.

Luke asked, "How's our gunshot target, our pin cushion for lead? Is Freddy recovering – no long term damage to his brain?"

Smiling, Gregorio responded, "Thank goodness the last shot hit him on his hard head. He's been shot three times now. He said that enough is enough."

"And what is Carmen, your mom, going to do?"

"She's going home to visit family in Mexico. Freddy and I are going to build her another cabin on our parcel. She'll be back in about four months when we're finished."

About an hour later, Alyce came over and hugged Gregorio. She said, "You know that she's in heaven. She's at rest. Any time you want to talk about anything, please feel free to drop by. The coffee pot is always on."

He nodded and forced another smile.

She spoke softly to Luke and said, "Joanna is taking care of JJ and Margarita, and my mother. Let's say our 'goodbyes' and 'thank yous.' I believe it is time to start our honeymoon."

Luke said, "*Adios mi hermano.* We will never forget Abby. She was a very special woman."`

Gregorio hugged them both. He said, "*Vaya con Dios, mis Amigos.*"

Off they went, hand in hand, turning the page and beginning another chapter of the story of Arizona...

Old West Scribblings

THE COWBOY'S DREAM

Last night as I lay on the prairie,
And looked to the stars in the sky,
And I wondered if ever a cowboy
Could drift to that sweet by and by.
The road to that bright happy region,
Is a dim narrow trail, so they say;
But the broad one that leads to perdition
Is posted and blazed along the way.
They say there will be a great roundup
And cowboys like doggies will stand
To be cut by the riders of Judgment
Who are posted and know every brand.
I wonder if ever a cowboy
Stood ready for the Judgment day,
And could say to the boss riders,
I'm ready – come drive me away.

INDIAN PRAYER

O' Great Spirit
Whose voice I hear in the wind
And whose breath gives life
To all the world, hear me!
I am small and weak,
I need your strength and wisdom.
Let me walk in beauty,
And make my eyes ever behold
The red and purple sunset.

Make my hands respect the things you have made,
And ears able to hear your voice.
Make me wise,
So that I may understand
The things you have taught my people.

HUNGRY DOGS HANGING OUT

Three dogs sat on the sidewalk
Outside the butcher shop
With drooling mouths and pleading eyes,
But no one slowed or stopped.
Waiting for the butchered goods
They lounged there in the street.
They got their stare of hostile stares
But not a shred of meat.
"I can't handle this, the town dog said,
"I'm gonna slip inside
And steal a steak and eat it
'Till my hunger's satisfied.
The ranch dog said, "You go ahead
And burgle, swipe and steal,
But rustlin' goes against the Code,
Not even for a meal."
"My credit's good down at the bank
I've got some equity,
I'll get a loan. I'll go in hock
To pay the butcher's fee."
The town dog and the ranch dog said,
"What's you gonna do?"
To the third one of the trio,
A farm dog named Ole Blue.
Ole Blue said, "Ain't going to steal,
And I ain't about to borrow,
'Cause either way, you must pay
The piper comes tomorrow.
If you're lookin' fer a handout,

Here's a trick that works plumb fine,
Be patient and look downhearted,
But most important – whine!"

HAPPY TRAILS (song)

Some trails are happy ones,
Others are blue.
It's the way you ride the trail that counts,
Here's a happy one for you.
Happy trails to you until we meet again
Happy trails to you, keep smiling' until then.
Who cares about the clouds
When we're together?
Just sing a song and bring the sunny weather,
Happy trails to you 'till we meet again.

COWBOY TOAST

May you never lose a stirrup
May you never waste a loop
May you can stay full of syrup
An' your gizzard full of Whoop!

TO MY GUITAR

To you old friend of many moods,
Of strange and thrilling interludes;
I bid you rest behind the door,
'Cause I'm too tired to play some more.
And you old friend, don't seem to tire
And when I'm resting by the fire,
I hear you throbbing soft and sweet
Even tho' I'm sound asleep.
Your face is scratched and your neck is bent,
Your body patched with old cement;

How come, old pal, as years go by,
Your voice sounds better and mine sounds dry?
Now we've played together old pal for years,
At parties and dances, through laughter and tears;
You helped me and I helped you,
And together we lived, like God meant us to do.
Remember old pal, when you broke a string,
And you couldn't play and I couldn't sing;
Then came the time when my collie dog died,
And you dried my tears with a song when I cried.
So here's to you, old pal of mine,
Of shining rosewood, spruce and pine;
I hope when God picks out my star,
He'll let me keep my old guitar,

ROPE FEVER

Most cowboys will rope anything that wears fur,
From a newborn calf to a cinnamon bear.
There's even some cowpokes so full of rope spunk
They'll throw a quick loop on a little ol' skunk.
They may never give up likker
An' drink from the lake,
But ropin' one habit they just can't forsake.
The trouble they claim ain't in fillin' your noose
It's figurin' how to turn some critters loose.

THE WILD FLOWERS SPEAK

Walk softly and gently, oh creatures called men
As you enter our home in the canyon or glen;
Long months we have waited and this is the hour
To raise our heads proudly, to be loved as a flower.
You are welcome to stay here but please, be so kind
And not disturb us for here you will find,
A rest for the weary – a ballet of spring

As we dance in the wind and the meadowlarks sing.
Yes, this is the hour, so much we must do,
To paint the bare hillsides in yellow and blue;
So just rest and watch us – that's all that we ask,
Our time is so short and so mighty is our task.
Return to your houses and trains of steel
But leave us alone and your dreams will reveal,
A vision of flowers in canyon and glen.
Walk softly and gently, oh creatures called men.

HOME ON THE RANGE   (1876 song)

Oh, give me a home where the buffalo roam,
Where the deer and the antelope play,
Where seldom is heard a discouraging word,
And the kies are not cloudy all day.
Where the air so pure, the zephyrs so free,
The breezes is balmy and light,
That I would not exchange my home on the range
For all the cities so bright.
How often at night when the heavens are bright
With the light from the glittering stars,
How I stood here amazed and asked as I gazed,
If their glory exceeds that of ours.
Oh, I love these wild prairies where I roam
The curlews I love to hear scream
And I love the white rocks and the antelope flocks
That graze in the mountain-top green.
Oh, give me a land where the bright diamond sand
Flows leisurely down the stream
Where the graceful white swan goes sliding along
Like a maid in a heavenly dream.
Home, home on the range,
Where the deer and antelope play;
Where seldom is heard a discouraging word,
And the skies are not cloudy all day.

BE CAREFUL SON – BE CAREFUL DAD

It seems like only yesterday,
That I held his little hand;
And those little feet would stumble
Even on a grain of sand.
With patience never ending,
I would help him have his fun,
But 'oh' how many times I'd say
"Please be careful, son."
Those little legs grew stronger,
Why it seemed no time at all;
And my legs aren't no good no more,
At times I almost fall.
Then I hear those same old words,
At first it made me mad;
But it sure is a nice kinda feeling
When he says, "Please be careful, Dad."

JUST DO IT

Somebody said it couldn't be done
But he with a chuckle replied,
That maybe it couldn't, but he wouldn't be one
Who would say so 'till he had tried.
So he buckled right in with a trace of a grin
If he had worried, he done hid it.
He started to sing as he tackled the thing
That couldn't be done, and he did it.
Someone scoffed, "You'll never do that,
At least no one had ever done it."
But he took off his coat and took off his hat
And the first thing we knew, he'd begun it
With a lift of his chin and a bit of a grin,
Without any doubting or quiddit.
He started to sing as he tackled the thing
That couldn't be done, and he did it.

There are thousands to prophesy failure,
There are hundreds to point out to you, over and over,
The dangers that want to assail you;
But just buckle in with a bit of a grin.
Just take off your coat and go to it,
Just start to sing as you tackle the thing
That "cannot be done," and you'll do it!

SPECIAL APRON

When I used to visit Grandma,
I was very impressed,
By her all-purpose apron,
And the power it possessed.
She used it for a basket
When she gathered up the eggs
And flapped it as a weapon
When hens pecked at her feet and legs.
She used it for a hot pad
To remove a steaming pan
And when her brow was heated
She used it for a fan.
It dried our childish tears
When we scraped a knee and cry
And made a hiding place
When the little ones were shy.
Farm produce took in season
In the summer, spring and fall
Found its way into the kitchen
From Grandma's carry all.

THE OLD RED FOX (Ontario, Canada)

One cold November morning with a new snow on the ground,
I loaded up my scatter gun and whistled up my hound;
Waved goodbye to Lucille as I climbed up through the rocks,

And told her I'd be home that night with the hide of the old red fox.
Oh, the old red fox that lived on the hill,
He was laughin' and I guess he's laughin' still;
He led me quite a chase and he laughed right in my face,
The old red fox that lived on the hill.
We started out through Dundas and headed north for Guelph,
I didn't want to go that far but I couldn't help myself;
The hound dog tried to turn him and he sure could cover ground,
But I had to buy another pair of boots in Owen Sound.
He ran right through a barnyard as he headed up the Bruce,
My tongue was draggin' on the ground, my belt was getting' loose;
We had to stop for dinner underneath an old pine-tree,
The old fox ate ten chickens while I drank one cup of tea.
We thought we had him cornered when he headed for the Tub,
He only stopped a minute there to give his fleas a rub;
I let fly with 'Old Betsy' as he started on his way,
But he jumped inside the smoke-screen and swam across the bay.
Oh, the old red fox that lived on the hill,
He was laughin' and I guess he's laughin' still;
He led me quite a chase and he laughed right in my face,
The old red fox that lived on the hill.

ARIZONA WELCOME

Podner, yo're welcome to such as we've got,
The leaks in the roof - an' the beans in the pot,
The butter that's soft, an' the bunks that are hard,
The weeds that are growin' all over the yard.

Get up when yo're ready, be plumb at your ease,
Don't worry 'bout us, just do as yuh please,
Yuh don't have to thank us or laff at our jokes,
Sit deep - an' come often - yo're one of the folks.

Note: Unsigned writings above gathered from cowboy bars, napkins, postcards, dude ranches, even on bathroom walls in saloons, and on slips of paper and old envelopes scribbled on by Joe Race Sr., Gibson Race and Joe Race Jr.

Quotations:

(THAT MAKE YOU THINK)

<u>Alex Levine</u> – "Only Irish coffee provides in a single glass all four essential food groups: alcohol, caffeine, sugar and fat."

<u>Ben Franklin (1706-1790)</u> – "In wine there is wisdom, in beer there is freedom, in water there is bacteria."

<u>Buffalo Bill Cody (1846-1917)</u> – "What we want to do is give women more liberty than they have. Let them do any kind of work they see fit and if they do it as well as men, give them the same pay…"

<u>Butch Cassidy</u> to the Sundance Kid on survival – "You watch the trees…I'll watch the bushes…"

<u>Graffiti at Gym</u> – "Good health is merely the slowest possible rate at which one can die."

<u>Cicero – 55 BC</u> – "The budget should be balanced, the Treasury should be refilled, public debt should be reduced, the arrogance of officialdom should be tempered and controlled, and the assistance to foreign lands should be curtailed lest Rome becomes bankrupt. People must learn to work, instead of living on public assistance…"

<u>Cowboy Graffiti</u> – "If you find yourself in a hole, quit digging."

> "It's better to be a has-been than a never-was."

> "Don't squat with your spurs on."

> "When you lose, don't lose the lesson."

"Don't interfere with something that ain't bothering you none."

"Talk slowly, think quickly."

"Timing has a lot to do with the outcome of a rain dance."

"If it don't seem like it's worth the effort, it probably ain't."

"Always drink upstream from the herd."

"Tellin' a man to get lost and makin' him do it are two entirely different things."

"Sometimes you get, and sometimes you get got."

"When you're throwing your weight around, be ready to have it thrown around by someone else."

Haiku – Chiyo (1703-1775) – A morning glory twined round the bucket: I will ask my neighbor for water."

Henry James (1843-1916) at the Louvre – "The commodious ottoman had since been removed to the extreme regret of all weak-kneed lovers (arthritic) of the arts…"

Joe Namath – "When you win, nothing hurts!"

Jose Rizal (1861-1896) – "Two hands working together are better then a thousand clasped in prayer."

John Wayne (1907-1979) – "Tomorrow is the most important thing in life. Comes into us at midnight very clean. It's perfect when it arrives and it puts itself in our hands. It hopes we've learned something from yesterday."

King Edward VII (1841-1910) – "Duty is important but so too is fun. It don't matter what you do so long as you don't frighten the horses…"

Larry King – "I never learned anything while I was talking."

Margaret Thatcher – "Socialism is great – until you run out of other people's money."

Mark Twain (1835-1910) – "Suppose you were an idiot, and suppose you were a member of Congress... but then I repeat myself."

Martin Luther King Jr. (1929-1968) – "Freedom is never voluntarily given by the aggressor; it must be demanded by the oppressed..."

Norman Vincent Peale (1898-1993) – "I have two choices every day – either to be happy or be unhappy. What do think I do? I just choose to be happy, and that's all there is to it..."

Roy Rogers (1911-1998) – "When my time comes, just skin me and put me up on Trigger, just as though nothing had ever changed."

Saipan Graffiti – "A clear conscience is usually the sign of a bad memory."

"Behind every successful man is a woman. Behind the fall of a successful man is usually another woman."

"Women will never be equal to men until they can walk down the street with a bald head and a beer gut, and still think they are sexy."

Thomas Jefferson (1743-1826) – "A government big enough to give you everything you want, is strong enough to take everything you have..."

Thomas Mann (1875-1955) – "How shall a man live if he can no longer rely upon things turning out differently from what he thought?"

Winston Churchill (1874-1965) – "Don't worry about avoiding temptation. As you grow older, it will avoid you..."